Addie Malone, brave frontierswoman and founder of Shotgun Ridge in the 1800s, would be proud to see the town's bustling rebirth. Just last year, it was nearly extinct. But thanks to the efforts of four matchmaking old men, Shotgun Ridge is bursting at the family seams once more. Now it was time for a new bachelor roundup—and this time the town's preacher will be standing on the opposite side of the altar!

* * *

"Oh, right. It's every day that some nutty woman bursts into your life and asks you to marry her without even shaking your hand," Amy said.

Dan grinned. "Usually a marriage proposal prompts more than a handshake."

"That's just it. I don't know any of the rules. I have no earthly idea *how* to be a preacher's wife."

"Same as any other wife, I'd imagine."

"You're a minister!"

"Yes." His chocolate eyes went serious. So serious, she shivered. "I'm also a man."

Dear Reader,

Happy New Year! Harlequin American Romance is starting the year off with an irresistible lineup of four great books, beginning with the latest installment in the MAITLAND MATERNITY: TRIPLETS, QUADS & QUINTS series. In *Quadruplets on the Doorstep* by Tina Leonard, a handsome bachelor proposes a marriage of convenience to a lovely nurse for the sake of four abandoned babies.

In Mindy Neff's *Preacher's In-Name-Only Wife*, another wonderful book in her BACHELORS OF SHOTGUN RIDGE series, a woman must marry to secure her inheritance, but she hadn't counted on being an instant wife *and* mother when her new husband unexpectedly receives custody of an orphaned baby. Next, a brooding loner captivates a pregnant single mom in *Pregnant and Incognito* by Pamela Browning. These opposites have nothing in common—except an intense attraction that neither is strong enough to deny. Finally, Krista Thoren makes her Harlequin American Romance debut with *High-Society Bachelor*, in which a successful businessman and a pretty party planner decide to outsmart their small town's matchmakers by pretending to date.

Enjoy them all—and don't forget to come back again next month when a special three-in-one volume, *The McCallum Quintuplets*, featuring *New York Times* bestselling author Kasey Michaels, Mindy Neff and Mary Anne Wilson is waiting for you.

Wishing you happy reading,

Melissa Jeglinski
Associate Senior Editor
Harlequin American Romance

PREACHER'S IN-NAME-ONLY WIFE
Mindy Neff

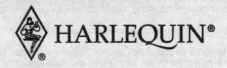

HARLEQUIN®

TORONTO • NEW YORK • LONDON
AMSTERDAM • PARIS • SYDNEY • HAMBURG
STOCKHOLM • ATHENS • TOKYO • MILAN • MADRID
PRAGUE • WARSAW • BUDAPEST • AUCKLAND

To Anne Jenkins
My high school pal and treasured friend.
I'm so proud of your accomplishments. You go, girl!

ISBN 0-373-16906-X

PREACHER'S IN-NAME-ONLY WIFE

ABOUT THE AUTHOR

Mindy Neff published her first book with Harlequin American Romance in 1995. Since then, she has appeared regularly on the Waldenbooks bestseller list and won numerous awards, including the National Readers' Choice Award and the *Romantic Times Magazine* Career Achievement Award.

Originally from Louisiana, Mindy settled in Southern California, where she married a really romantic guy and raised five great kids. Family, friends, writing and reading are her passions. When not writing, Mindy's ideal getaway is a good book, hot sunshine and a chair at the river's edge at her second home in Parker, Arizona.

Mindy loves to hear from readers and can be reached at P.O. Box 2704-262, Huntington Beach, CA 92647, or through her Web site at www.mindyneff.com, or e-mail at mindyneff@aol.com.

Books by Mindy Neff

HARLEQUIN AMERICAN ROMANCE

*Tall, Dark & Irresistible
†Bachelors of Shotgun Ridge

Don't miss any of our special offers. Write to us at the following address for information on our newest releases.

Harlequin Reader Service
U.S.: 3010 Walden Ave., P.O. Box 1325, Buffalo, NY 14269
Canadian: P.O. Box 609, Fort Erie, Ont. L2A 5X3

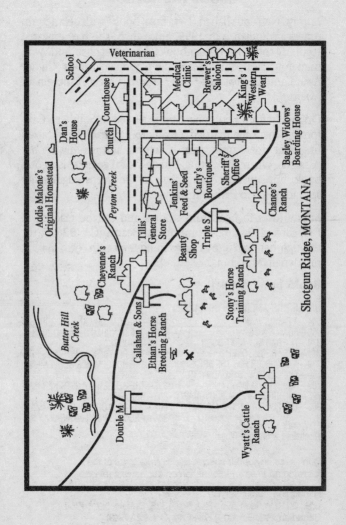

School

Veterinarian

Addie Malone's Original Homestead

Dan's House

Butter Hill Creek

Peyton Creek

Church

Courthouse

Medical Clinic

Brewer's Saloon

King's Western Wear

Bagley Widows' Boarding House

Jenkins' Feed & Seed

Carly's Boutique

Sheriff's Office

Chance's Ranch

Cheyenne's Ranch

Tillis' General Store

Beauty Shop

Triple S

Stony's Horse Training Ranch

Callahan & Sons

Ethan's Horse Breeding Ranch

Double M

Wyatt's Cattle Ranch

Shotgun Ridge, MONTANA

Prologue

Ozzie Peyton laid out his journal as he did every night, preparing to record his thoughts and feelings, but he hesitated before picking up his pen.

The logs in the fireplace crackled merrily. Above the mantel, he gazed at the portrait of his beautiful Vanessa. Each day he missed her even more. She was his rock, his conscience, his best friend and confidante—that she'd crossed over to the hereafter didn't change any of those facts.

Perhaps he was a crazy old man, but the bond between them seemed to grow stronger each day—not that he was about to *admit* that to anyone. Folks might start whispering about him losing his faculties, you bet. And that simply wasn't the case.

Now, his late friend, Ben Marshall, well, *there* was a shocking leave of absence from the senses, you bet.

He picked up his pen at last and began to write:

I must say, I never dreamed my conversation with my old buddy, Ben Marshall, would set such an unorthodox plan into action. Heck, when Ben called several months back, asking about Pastor

Dan Lucas and what type of a man he'd turned into, I'd been only too happy to expound on the boy's attributes. Maybe I shouldn't have been so puffed-up and shootin' my mouth off about this here matchmakin' venture me and the boys— that's Lloyd, Henry, Vern and me—have gotten into. So far, we're doing right well, even if I do say so myself. Woman and babies and happy families. Love is in the air, and that's as it should be.

Still, I like to have a little more control over matters, and my boasting just might have watered a seed that was planted years ago— watered it a little too good, is what I'm thinking. There are sure to be plenty of raised eyebrows in a few days' time.

He gazed up at his sweet Vanessa, then looked away to the inky blackness of a clear star-studded night beyond the window. Vanessa would probably have a thing or two to say on the subject of meddling in the preacher's life. Not that Ozzie himself had precisely been the one to meddle—more's the pity he hadn't thought of it first.

Then again, it was risky business taking credit for the events that were already set in motion. The ramifications of it backfiring were huge.

Ozzie licked the tip of his Bic pen and set it to the paper again.

I tell you, I could hardly sit still in the sermon this morning at church. It's clear as day that

Dan Lucas considers himself safe from matchmaking, but preachers need love and happily-ever-after, too, you bet. After all, the boy is always insisting he's simply a man—albeit a man with a message to tell and a gift for gab and showmanship.

Still, I never imagined my old buddy, Ben, would up and die on us suddenly, or that he'd wave that fool betrothal agreement in everyone's faces this way. Why it was a boyhood pact, for goodness' sake, a lark, easily forgotten.

Matchmaking and being on hand to watch the fireworks is one thing. Doing it from the grave is quite another. I figure me and the boys'll need to keep a close eye on this here shebang. I just hope like heck my buddy, Ben, didn't make a big mistake.

Chapter One

It wasn't often that Dan Lucas found himself with time on his hands. As the minister in the small town of Shotgun Ridge, Montana, his days were constantly filled with people. Oh, he enjoyed it. Immensely. He wouldn't trade his life here for anything.

Each day brought changes and new challenges. He derived great satisfaction from seeing his friends find what they were searching for in life—Wyatt, Ethan, Stony, Cheyenne and Chance had all married and started families within the past year or so. Dan had gone to school with all of them, raised some Cain and gotten into his fair share of trouble with them, too, before he'd settled into his own calling.

They had a history, he and these people of Shotgun Ridge. A bond. More than a few people had been surprised when he'd decided to follow his father into the ministry.

He supposed getting a DUI citation while driving old man Grisby's tractor might have fueled that surprise.

Most days Dan considered himself content. More than content. Then others, he felt a pang. He didn't spend a lot of time questioning or worrying, though. The future wasn't in his hands.

The afternoon, however, *was*. Amazingly, he was free for the next six hours.

He looked out the back window of the medical clinic to the empty parking lot beyond. The patient he'd stopped in to see had left, and so had the doctors, Kelly and Chance Hammond. Needing to make a couple of phone calls, he'd made use of the clinic's phone rather than walk back across the street to the church office, and promised to lock up on his way out. As a rule, folks didn't lock their doors here in Shotgun Ridge, but since the clinic housed drugs, it was the exception.

Before he shut the blinds, he gave a wave to Eddie Housen, who was riding around in his snowplow, looking for stray patches of snow to scrape. Eddie had gotten a new scoop for the front of his two-ton pickup and, like a kid on Christmas morning, was itching to use it. Too bad the weather wasn't cooperating. Bits of snow still clung to the ground and piled in muddy mounds of slush along the roadside, but they hadn't had any new snowfall in over a week.

Dan laughed out loud at the forlorn look on the man's face. Nothing worse than having a new piece of machinery and not being able to have any fun with it. If there'd been icy snow on the ground, Dan might have been tempted to hitch a ride with Eddie and see if the guy would let him have a turn at the wheel.

But he had other plans. Anticipating a much-needed date with a certain chestnut gelding in the stable across the road at his ranch house behind the church, Dan closed the door of the back office and started down the hall. He could already imagine the brisk winter air on his cheeks, biting at his ears beneath his Stetson, sneaking beneath the cuffs of his leather gloves.

Montana in the winter was misery to some, but Dan loved it.

The sound of paper crinkling and a chair scraping across the floor alerted him that he was no longer alone in the clinic. He thought maybe Kelly and Chance had forgotten something. Since they weren't expecting any more patients, they'd gone over to Brewer's Saloon for a late lunch.

Curious, he headed toward the front of the clinic. The smell of antiseptic and alcohol permeated the air, a far cry from the scents of aged wood and lemon oil associated with the church. Different, yet still familiar since he'd spent many, many hours in clinics and hospitals comforting the sick and dying—or their families.

When he didn't see anyone waiting in the reception area, he glanced into one of the examining rooms he passed, and nearly tripped over his own boots.

He'd heard his pals talking about being poleaxed by the sight of a woman.

He'd never understood the term until just now.

She wore laced-up hiking boots, jeans that were frayed at the hem from scraping against the heel, a white T-shirt tucked in at the waist with a man's flannel shirt unbuttoned and hanging loose over it. A cloud of rich dark hair brushed her shoulders with the gleaming chestnut highlights that put him in mind of his gelding's healthy shining coat.

In contrast to her casual clothing, her flawless skin and killer bone structure made him think of a fashion model. She was the kind of woman whose striking features would turn heads and cause any red-blooded man to develop a stutter, even if she were wearing a burlap feed sack.

The thought that ran through his head was a cliché for sure, but he couldn't get past it.

She was simply the most beautiful woman he'd come across in ages.

"Can I help you?" Thank God, he didn't have a stuttering problem.

She jumped at the sound of his voice. Her eyes went liquid with tears, yet her chin jutted out. Overwhelmed, he surmised, yet fighting it. He'd counseled enough people to recognize the signs.

"There was no nurse outside, and I was feeling faint, so I just came in here to wait. I hope that's all right."

Her accent signaled she was from the Deep South, Georgia or Tennessee, he guessed. "Sure...the nurse, uh, stepped out." Actually, Kelly Hammond was a doctor, rather than a nurse. "You said you were feeling faint—?"

Before he could finish his sentence, or put a plan of action together to get some help over here, she nodded and launched into speech.

"It's probably nothing that a firing squad aimed at my grandfather wouldn't cure. If he hadn't just passed on, he'd be fearing for his health at *my* hands, that's for darn sure.''

"I'm sorry for your loss," Dan murmured. Although genuine pain shadowed her expressive green eyes, she appeared not to hear him.

"I swear I've had it up to here." Her hand made a slicing motion at the level of her brow. "I don't know what's wrong with me lately—well, I probably do, but that's beside the point. Then again, you're a doctor, so maybe it's not really beside the point."

Uh-oh.

"I think my brain's on overload. Life has simply thrown me too many curves in too short of a time. I haven't been eating like I should, I know. Maybe it's hormones. Between you and me, doc to patient, I haven't had *sex* in longer than I can remember. I mean, who has time with all the stuff I've had to deal with?" She rambled on without stopping, her hands keeping time with her words and punctuating her sentences like a distraught mime playing to an audience of critics.

Dan knew he should probably interrupt. Under the circumstances, it would be polite.

He opened his mouth to do so but wasn't quick enough.

"And if that doesn't make me feel low enough to jump off a dime, *now* I've been shooed off to a town I've never even heard of, where I'm supposed to propose marriage to the *preacher!*"

Dan nearly swallowed his tongue. He was a man rarely at a loss for words. For the life of him, he couldn't seem to form the ones needed to head off the disaster playing out before him.

"Can you *imagine?* No wonder I'm feeling dizzy. Do you think it's hormonal? Does that cause you to feel light-headed?"

Well...hmm. This was tricky. He cleared his throat, leaned a shoulder against the wall, tried like crazy not to smile—or choke. He was actually sweating and it was a cool sixty-five degrees in the clinic.

"Um, I can't honestly say...since I'm not the doctor. I'm the preacher."

Her eyes widened as though she'd just seen Martha Stewart drop-kick a salmon.

"*You're* the preacher?"

"'Fraid so."

"Of *this* town?"

"Mmm-hmm."

"The *only* one?"

"Guilty."

She leaped down off the examining table, snatched up her oversize backpack purse and clutched it to her chest like a shield. "How could you just stand there and let me run off at the mouth that way?"

"You didn't give me much opportunity to do otherwise."

"I thought you were the doctor. My God, I told you I hadn't had sex!"

Yes, and he shouldn't have found that quite so interesting. "You wouldn't be the first to confide such a detail."

Amy Marshall covered her face with one hand. She was mortified. That's all there was to it. It was bad enough that she was on this ridiculously unorthodox mission in the first place. And because she felt embarrassed, that made her mad.

Vulnerability and feeling helpless were emotions she did her level best to avoid.

She swore, then cut off the word in mid-syllable when she belatedly realized who she'd just cursed at. The day was going from bad to worse.

Unable to think of a smart comeback, she leveled him with a mutinous look. Talk about feeling faint. Heat coursed through her body, her heart was beating fast, and vertigo was really trying to get the better of her now.

Her only thought was to flee. Regroup. She wasn't prepared. She needed time to plan her words, present her case in a reasonable, logical manner.

If such a thing were even possible.

Good Lord. She'd been willing to undress before this man, tell him every intimate detail. That's what one did in a doctor's office. There was a certain expected, unquestioned trust involved in entering a medical establishment.

Usually.

"Being celibate's not such a terrible thing, is it?" he asked, the corners of his lips curving ever so slightly.

"For you, maybe." She slammed her mouth shut before she dug herself into a deeper mess. Admitting to a preacher that she was sexually frustrated was simply too much for her overwhelmed brain to handle.

The very preacher she was here to propose to.

Gripping her backpack that held a small fortune in

camera equipment she never went anywhere without, she tried to storm past him.

He reached out and gently touched her arm, his smile gone, his features concerned. A blinding burst of heat shot through her like the brilliant strobe of her Nikon speed-light flash.

That upset her even more.

She stiffened and he immediately dropped his hands.

''Maybe we should introduce ourselves?''

She merely stared at him. She'd never been so horrified in her entire life. *Of course* they should introduce themselves. That's what she was here for—well, not here at this exact moment, but still. She'd come to find him. A polite, civilized exchange of names was in order.

Instead, she wished fervently for a nice hole to gape open in the drab tile floor and swallow her up.

She'd rambled on like a person who didn't have sense enough to pour rainwater out of a boot. And heaven above, this man was gorgeous. He was nothing like she'd expected, nothing like she'd pictured.

She'd expected him to be, oh…nerdy, perhaps. He was as far from nerdy as a Kodak Instamatic was from a Nikon F5. This man topped her five-foot-six height by a good eight inches, had shoulders better suited to a linebacker, and could give Matthew McConaughey—one of her most fantasized about movie idols—a run for his money in the sex appeal department.

Cryin' all night, he looked like a mouthwatering

cowboy in those pointy-toed boots, faded jeans and a Stetson clutched loosely in one hand.

Where the heck was his clerical collar? A robe? Something. Anything to give her a clue he was a minister and not just a guy in Western clothes with more than his fair share of good looks?

And darn it all, he had no business being *her* preacher!

"Why don't we start over. My name's Dan Lucas."

"I know that *now.*"

"Then you have me at a disadvantage."

"Maybe I like it that way." She wasn't normally given to petulance. At the moment it was nearly impossible to suppress the emotion.

He laughed. The sound reverberated around the room, wrapped around the corners, invaded her insides, invited participation.

She wasn't going to get suckered in. But she couldn't stand here and not reciprocate introductions. It was time to take control.

"Amy Marshall." If he expected her to hold out her hand and indulge in another of those lightning flashes of heat at the touch of their skin, he'd have to think again.

Oh, for heaven's sake, Amy. The man's a minister. He's not thinking about sex.

She waited to see if her name drew a spark of recognition, but he didn't respond, merely watched her, quietly, carefully, gently.

"Doesn't ring any bells?"

"I'm sorry. I have a feeling it should since you say

you're here to…um, propose. Maybe you could give
me a few more details and we can go from there?''

Oh, she had plenty of details, murky and outrageous as they were. But a streak of cowardice shot
straight up her spine. ''Later, okay? Right now, I need
some time to regroup.'' She ducked her head, tried to
inch past him.

''Amy.'' He stepped into her path, stopping her.
On any other man, the action could have been con-
strued as threatening.

His wide shoulders were within touching distance.
She could smell the crisp scent of winter on his
clothes, the lingering trace of shampoo in his hair.
Scents that would alert an animal in the wild to the
presence of a human, and possibly danger—reasons
Amy herself never wore perfume.

She felt those danger flags now, as though she were
the cornered animal, unsure whether to choose flight
or fight.

''Look, I'm more embarrassed than you can imagine right now.''

''There's no need. I'm as much to blame—even
more. I should have told you I wasn't the doctor right
away.''

She could tell he genuinely felt bad and decided to
give him a break. ''As you so aptly pointed out, I
didn't give you much chance. It's a failing of mine.
I tend to go at mach speed, and I don't stop to think.''

''All the more reason you should wait for the doctor. You ought to let Chance Hammond check you
over. He and his wife Kelly are the doctors here in
town. They'll be back in a few minutes.''

"Forget it. After this mortifying experience, there's no telling what I'll say or do."

"There has to be a reason for feeling faint. I'm no doctor—"

She raised her brows, and his answering smile gave her a swift, tingling punch in the solar plexus.

"I'd still feel better if you'd wait."

But she wouldn't. Her nerves were jumping like a frog in a frying pan and her brain was screaming for action. They were instincts she'd relied on all her life to keep her on track. She was no southern belle damsel-in-distress. Control, drive and determination would keep her self-reliant.

Unlike her mother.

Though she loved her mother dearly, she refused to fall into the same trap Chandra Marshall had. Without skills, dependent upon others.

That was probably the biggest rub in this whole ridiculous mission. Amy, herself, had no control. Her mother's future lay squarely in the hands of the preacher facing her.

He was still watching her in that quiet way of his, steadily, intensely, a look that made her heart pump and her palms go damp. It was a ridiculous reaction. He was simply concerned.

When in the world had she begun seeing sensuality in compassion? she asked herself.

Ten minutes ago, was the answer. The instant she'd laid eyes on this man. The man who could alter her entire future with a simple word. *Yes* or *no*.

Had there been a divine hand in all this? *Oh, for heaven's sake.* The good Lord above didn't go around smiting women with dizzy spells so they'd bump into preachers they were supposed to propose to.

"I feel fine now, Dan. More than likely I just need to eat something. I've been on the road for almost a week, and I haven't stopped regularly for meals."

"I can help you there." He went to his jacket, pulled a candy bar out of the pocket and handed it to her. "I keep it for the kids."

She pounced on the chocolate like a greedy child at a backyard picnic.

He chuckled. "Maybe you'll let me buy you something more substantial over at Brewer's?"

"Mmm." She licked her fingers. Now that her taste buds were fully awake, she realized that she was actually starving. "I'd kill for a greasy hamburger right about now. I didn't notice any local fast-food joints."

"You're in luck. Brewer's serves the best burgers this side of heaven."

She couldn't help but give him a cocky smile. "Coming from an authority like you, they must be good. Just point me in the right direction."

"I'm going that way. Why don't I buy?"

"I don't need you to buy me a meal."

"Oh, you just need me to marry you."

The words dropped neatly into a pocket of silence. She choked on the last swallow of candy.

His laughter rang out again. "Sorry, I couldn't resist. I confess, I'm highly intrigued when a beautiful woman comes to town claiming a need to propose to me. My curiosity's going to keep me up. Maybe we should talk?"

He wasn't taking her seriously, and she fully understood why. Who could blame him? She wished to heaven this *was* all a big joke.

But it wasn't. And she couldn't give in to the cowardly instincts begging her to stall. Sooner or later they'd have to talk. Might as well be now.

"Fine. My Jeep's out front. Want me to drive?"

"Sure you're up to it? I don't want you passing out and running us in a ditch."

"How far are we going?"

"Half a block."

"I think I can manage to keep us on the road for half a block."

BREWER'S SALOON WAS a cozy diner, with a bar off to one side, vinyl booths and tables topped with red-checked cloths, and a jukebox playing a lively country-and-western tune.

Dan leaned down close to her ear. "The doc and his wife are sitting right over there. Sure you don't want to go have a talk with them?"

She turned her head, dismayed to find her lips practically touching his. "Food is all I need, thank you."

And a husband for ninety days.

"Right. A greasy burger. I'm thinking you're the kind of woman who goes for the fully loaded variety, onions and all."

"And what do you base that on?"

"Your self-proclaimed tendencies to go at mach speed. Type-A personality, curious, adventurous. Am I close?"

Entirely *too* close. Both in his assessment and in his proximity. "I had no idea preachers were smug."

He laughed and the sound drew heads around, along with answering smiles and waves. Besides the doctor and his wife, there were only two other customers in the diner, as well as an older woman behind the bar and another serving food.

Amy could feel their curiosity as though she was freeze-framed in the focus of a high-powered zoom lens. It wasn't an uncomfortable awareness. It was just…there.

Dan waved back, called a few hellos, then led her into the back room through a set of swinging doors where a group of older men were playing billiards and watching each other's shots like hustlers who'd managed to slip past the tournament rules.

"It's actually more private back here," he said, obviously feeling the need to explain why they'd bypassed the open booths out front. "And I can indulge in a cigar now and again without Iris Brewer pitching a fit."

Amy's jaw dropped at that piece of news, but her attention was snagged when the white-haired man with the cue stick scratched his shot, causing the three other old fellows to whoop and jest.

As though a signal had passed silently between the four men, they all looked up and over at Dan and Amy.

"Afternoon, Pastor Dan," the apparent leader of the bunch said, his vivid blue eyes homing in on Amy.

Dan laughed, a sound that was still jolting, yet becoming familiar.

"Ozzie," Dan acknowledged. With a hand at

Amy's back, he urged her over toward the pool table. "You boys betting again?"

"Durn straight," Ozzie said, clearly unrepentant in the presence of the preacher. "And I'm paddin' my retirement fund right nicely, even if I do say so myself. You bet. Who've we got here?"

"Amy Marshall," Dan introduced. "Meet Ozzie Peyton, our esteemed mayor and general all-around meddler. His sidekicks here are Lloyd Brewer—he owns this place—Vern Tillis from the general store and Henry Jenkins, who keeps our livestock and crops fed and healthy."

Ozzie laid aside his cue stick and took one of Amy's hands in both of his, his striking blues eyes filled with compassion and something more.

"I knew your grandfather. We served together in the war. He was a good man, always had the best of intentions, you bet. I'm mighty sorry over his passing."

Automatically she nodded her thanks. *Always had the best of intentions,* he'd said.

Amy was a trained watcher. She had to be to wait out skittish or difficult photography subjects, wait until the right moment, the right atmosphere to get a perfect shot. She didn't miss the slight shift in the older man's gaze as he took in both her and Dan at the same time.

Did he know about the will?

Then his name clicked in her mind. The attorney had mentioned Ozzie Peyton when he'd been giving her instructions along with directions to Shotgun Ridge.

She remembered shutting down about that time, too overwhelmed at the chaos of her life to pay much attention, too stunned that she'd actually been maneuvered into taking this step in the first place, agreeing to the crazy terms of the well-meaning, obviously nutty man she'd loved dearly.

She felt Dan's hand slide around her waist, a clear gesture of support, and sensed him watching her. She gave him a smile to let him know she wasn't in danger of fainting, even if her insides were trembling like a quiet brook rippled by a gusty breeze.

"If you boys'll excuse us, Amy's had a long drive and is in need of sustenance."

"Of course. You bet. Lloyd'll go run down Maedean and get her in here to take your orders."

"Just tell her to bring out two burger specials with the works," Dan said, leading Amy to a booth.

A woman came through the swinging doors with a pitcher of water and two glasses. "I'll take care of it, dear," she said to Lloyd.

As Amy slid into the booth, the woman set the glasses and pitcher on the table, then wiped her hand on her apron and held it out. "I'm Iris Brewer. Part owner of this joint, wife to that old coot over there and all-around grandma to the little ones in town."

Amy smiled. She liked this woman in an instant. Friendly, motherly, *capable*. Iris's hand was small but surprisingly strong in Amy's grip.

"Amy Marshall," she said.

"You're new..." She laughed. "Well, of course you are. Silly of me to point out the obvious. Will you be staying long?"

Heat crept up Amy's face. She didn't blush often. In her secondary line of work, she'd gotten over that trait in the first week.

Before she could think of a good answer, Iris backtracked. "Oh, that was rude of me. You're probably starving half to death and here I go with twenty questions. You kids just get settled in, and I'll go rustle up those hamburgers. That'll put you right and at ease in no time at all."

She bustled away, and Amy felt acutely embarrassed. Dan was watching her and her nerves were screaming. All this over a silly, telltale blush.

She took a sip of water, then looked across the table at Dan. The older men had gone back to their pool game, and Amy felt comfortable that their conversation would indeed remain private.

"I have no idea where to start."

"Anywhere's fine. I'm pretty adept at jumping in at most any point and keeping up."

"I suppose you get a lot of people telling you their troubles?"

"A few. Are you going to tell me your troubles?"

"It'd be the kind thing to do since you're a big part of them. Oh, that didn't come out right. But the mess I'm in could affect you, too."

He leaned back in the booth, gave her his attention. "I'm all yours."

Oh, buddy, you have no idea how those words are about to bite you in the butt.

"Though we've obviously never met," she said, "I guess the two of us have somewhat of a past."

He raised a brow, and she lost her train of thought.

The man poured more sex appeal into a simple gesture than most men could manage in an entire, well thought out seduction. The blood hummed in her veins and her hands trembled.

This was going to be much more difficult than she'd imagined. And she'd already imagined a great deal of difficulty.

"A past?" he prompted.

"Our fathers went to college together at Georgia Tech and for some crazy reason, they made a betrothal pact to marry off their firstborn kids."

Dan chuckled. "Amy, my dad's a minister. I can't imagine him doing something like that. And besides, a boyhood pact isn't a legally binding document."

She glared at him. She'd had the same flippant, dismissing attitude herself; disbelieving, brushing the idea off as ludicrous, not worthy of a second thought.

All that had changed when Gramps's attorney had forcibly sat her down, made her listen, heaped a responsibility on her shoulders she wanted nothing to do with.

"I'm only telling you what I know. I didn't say it was sane. Do you want to hear this or not?"

With obvious skepticism, he nodded. "I'm listening."

Chapter Two

Amy took a breath and gathered her thoughts. She'd gotten off to a bad start.

"I don't remember my father ever mentioning yours, so I'm assuming they might have lost contact over the years. My dad, Mark Marshall, died twelve years ago, so I can't ask him."

Dan reached across the table and laid his hand briefly atop her. "How old were you then?"

"Seventeen. I'm twenty-nine, now." Clever way to ferret out her age, she thought. "And you?"

"Thirty-two. I'll ask my father if he can fill in any history blanks."

"Is he local, then?"

"By phone. They're down in Sheridan, Wyoming."

She nodded. She'd like to meet the man who'd made such a pact, ask him why. "It's hard to say if Dad kept in touch with friends. He was a photographer, away from home a lot." She traced a finger through stray granules of spilled sugar on the table. "Gramps didn't approve."

"That's a shame—that your father didn't have his parents' approval."

"He did what he loved best, though. He followed his dream."

"He died young?"

"Yes. An injury that kept nagging at him. He went in for routine—or what they said was routine—back surgery and didn't make it off the operating table." She liked the comfort Dan's touch brought as he squeezed her fingers in compassion, but it was also distracting. She pulled her hand back.

"Dad never got around to things like life insurance, so his death left my mom in a mess. Thankfully Gramps stepped in and paid off the mortgage on the house. My mom had always been a wife and mother. She didn't have any outside skills to bring in an income...and didn't have the drive or desire to acquire them."

"You were lucky, then, to have your grandfather."

"He was a big influence in my life."

"Something tells me you didn't let him run it, though."

"No, which is probably why he's trying to do it from the grave. I adored Gramps, but I was determined to pull my own weight. I didn't want to be one of those rich kids who lived on an allowance and bided her time till the day she could get her hands on a trust fund."

Iris returned and set baskets of burgers and fries in front of them, patted Dan affectionately on the shoulder, then left them to their privacy.

"I loved photography," Amy said, smothering the

fries and burger with half a bottle of ketchup. "From the minute I looked through the viewfinder of my dad's first Hasselblad, I was hooked. Gramps didn't approve of that as a career choice for me any more than he had for Dad, but he thought I'd outgrow it."

She paused for a moment to savor the burger, closed her eyes and nearly moaned, then scooped up her napkin to wipe her mouth. "Oh, my gosh, these are great."

"Brewer's make the best."

"So you said. I'll remember to pay attention to your restaurant recommendations in the future. Anyway, I went to college, got a degree in journalism and worked at the local paper for a while, but I wanted to travel, record life on frames of film—unique images that most people missed or never got a chance to see. To pit myself against the elements and get the perfect shot." To search for that one Pulitzer Prize winning photo that would validate the career choice her father had made.

"It's a rush, you know? Watching the images take shape on the developed film, capturing every nuance of character and place. Vivid. Real. In order to travel, though, I needed money. And I didn't want to take it from Gramps."

"There's nothing wrong with accepting a gift given in love from a family member."

"I wasn't being stubborn at that point. Gramps wouldn't have funded my traveling dreams. He didn't approve of Dad doing it, and he wanted more from me."

He laid aside his hamburger and studied her. "So what did you do?"

"I went to work as a cocktail waitress to save money."

"Mmm."

What did he mean by that "mmm"? "It paid well," she defended.

"Well enough to travel?"

"Um...this particular establishment did." She pushed aside her own burger and gave him a direct look, wondering if she was about to shock him. "I worked at a gentleman's club."

He barely blinked. But proving that he was indeed a man, his eyes dipped for a split instant to her chest, then right back to her eyes.

She waited to see if he'd acknowledge the typically male reaction, apologize. But he just looked at her steadily, without an ounce of repentance.

"Did you...?"

"Strip?" She laughed. Because that, too, was typically male. "No. I only waitressed."

"Go on."

"Gramps came in one night—"

"To the strip club?"

"It wasn't a seedy joint, Dan."

"Sorry. I didn't mean to judge."

"Anyway, he didn't know I worked there, and he flipped."

"Mmm."

"Would you stop saying that?"

His lips twitched on a smile he was wise enough to suppress. "Go on."

"He ranted and raved and wanted me to quit on the spot. When I got home, he'd tried to enlist my mom's influence, and was even more annoyed that she knew where I worked and stood up for me. He left in a huff, muttering about changing his will. I figured that was fine. I didn't want his money. I had plans of my own. If he cut me out of his will, it wasn't going to make me love him any less."

She paused and took a sip of water, then dragged a now soggy French fry back and forth through a pool of ketchup.

"I never imagined he'd cut my *mother* out of the will—or she will be out unless I honor this betrothal pact our fathers made."

He shifted in his seat. She didn't blame him for being uncomfortable. She was fairly squirming herself.

"Specifically, what did the will say?"

She reached into her purse and withdrew a document. "I have a copy here for you to read—the portion that pertains to the two of us. The paraphrased version is that I marry you or my mother's home will be sold and the proceeds donated to charity."

She pushed the papers across the table. "And before you ask me about the legalities, I covered every angle I know of with the attorney. Gramps could do anything he wanted with his assets. The codicil is legal and binding—even if it's outrageous."

She watched as he skimmed the document. The overhead lights caught the coffee-colored highlights in his thick dark hair. A Stetson lay on the vinyl seat beside him. His hands were large, his forearms muscular. He had a physique better suited to a tough wrangler than a minister whose power would radiate from a pulpit rather than from horseback.

"The attorney is named as executor," he said after a long moment.

"He'd need to see a marriage certificate."

"Within a month." He glanced up. "Your grandfather was gambling a lot on your and your mother's future."

"More than you know."

He frowned. "And that means?"

"Look, Dan. I don't want to be here any more than you want me here—"

"I don't believe I said anything about not wanting you here."

"Oh, right. It's every day that some nutty woman bursts into your life, blurts out her sexual woes and asks you to marry her without even shaking your hand."

He grinned, then laughed. "Usually a marriage proposal prompts more than a handshake."

"We're total strangers."

"People do usually get acquainted before they marry," he concluded.

"That's just it. I don't know any of the rules. I have no earthly idea *how* to be a preacher's wife." Flustered, she hadn't meant to blurt that out.

His brows rose a fraction of an inch. "Same as any other wife, I'd imagine."

She nearly pounded her fist against the Formica tabletop, despite the fact that she was a nervous wreck. "And I suppose you're an authority on the subject?"

"Not an authority, since I've never been married. Just for the sake of argument, what's your main objection?"

"You're a minister!"

He shrugged. "Yes." His chocolate eyes went serious and intent. So serious, she shivered.

"I'm also a man." For a long, charged moment he held her gaze. Then he raked a hand through his hair. "I don't know why I'm defending myself or leading the conversation in this direction. You proposed to me, if I remember correctly."

"Under duress," she muttered.

"As a minister, I make it a rule never to marry a couple under duress."

"I don't have a choice. I don't like this any better than you do. It couldn't have come at a worse time." She had a horrified thought that she might be insulting him and quickly backtracked.

"I mean, you seem like a really nice man. You're handsome and have a great laugh, and any woman would be..." What? she wondered. Overjoyed at the thought of going to bed with this sexy guy?

She couldn't very well say that. Especially since all she wanted was an official piece of paper.

She didn't want the trappings that came with the marriage.

And that was the biggest problem of all. The guilt she felt for putting him in this position of accepting or turning her down was huge. He didn't owe her a thing. He didn't know her from Adam—or Eve as the case may be.

"Any woman would be what?" he prompted.

"Never mind. If it was just me, I wouldn't be here. But my mom's whole way of life is at stake. She doesn't have job skills. And neither one of us has enough savings to get her set up in another place."

"You said this was a bad time for you?"

She nodded, feeling her stomach tighten, her heart pump. "Two days after Gramps died, I got a job offer from *National Geographic*. I've been periodically sending them samples of my work, and they'd seen a piece I'd won a local award for. It's the chance of a lifetime." A chance even her father hadn't been offered.

This job would allow her to follow in her father's footsteps, to walk forward from where he'd left off, to keep his memory alive. To prove that holding on to a coveted dream was worth the personal sacrifice it often entailed.

Most people, her grandfather specifically, could only condone sacrifices if there were tangible or glamorous results, evidence that the fruits of the dogged pursuit were worthy—like a lucrative payment, a world-recognized byline…an acclaimed award. Anything else, in his opinion, had merely been considered a hobby.

"And if you go, your mother loses her home."

"Yes and no. Actually, they've offered to hold the job open for ninety days."

"Long enough to comply with the terms of your grandfather's will."

She looked at him, nodded, didn't bother to keep the pleading out of her eyes, or the sorrow and guilt. "I know you've probably got moral issues with this whole thing. I know *I* do, and I'm not the minister of a church. But I have to do this for my mom."

"What does she think of this…?"

"Craziness? She's hurt that Gramps would do such a thing."

"Did they not get along?"

"That's just the thing. They got along great. He teased her about being a Yankee, but he treated her like a daughter. It doesn't make a lot of sense."

"So, your mother supported your decision to come here?"

"Outwardly, no. But inwardly…that house has been her home for thirty years. It's a part of her, the grounds, her gardens. It's a beautiful old plantation home on six acres of land that's seen many an afternoon tea party. She's part of the town, part of that house. It's all she knows and loves. She doesn't know how to be anything except lady of her manor." It was difficult to explain her mother. Chandra Marshall was…delicate.

She sighed and curled her fingers into her palms until the short, neatly trimmed nails cut into her palm. "I'm asking a lot, I know." She didn't know what else to say. "Please think about it."

The compassion in his eyes made her stomach lurch. He had every right to turn her down. Any sane person would. She couldn't let him, would beg if necessary. "It's only for ninety days. It wouldn't be…we wouldn't…you know."

"Consummate the union?"

She'd blushed more times in the last two hours than she had in the past two years. "Yes. I mean, no! We wouldn't do that."

"What *would* we do?"

Was he deliberately being difficult? Baiting her? "Live together as friends, I guess. Is that so hard to picture? Haven't you ever had a roommate?"

"Not one I was married to."

The frustration was overwhelming her. Tears stung the back of her eyes, clogged her throat. She fought them like crazy. She would *not* fall apart. She would *not* be weak.

Like her mother.

The unexpected thought ricocheted and smacked her in the solar plexus. She loved her mother.

"Hey," Dan said, reaching across the table.

She shook her head. "I'm okay. I'm just tired. I'm acting like such a…a *female*."

He chuckled. "I'm glad to hear it. Wouldn't want you acting like a *male*."

That actually brought a laugh bubbling to the surface.

"Men don't cry," she agreed.

"Well, I don't know about that. I've been known to a time or two, and I'm definitely a male."

She imagined he hadn't intended his comment to be a sexual one, but it struck her that way. All she had to do was look at him and the word "male" blazed in her mind like neon on a theater sign.

What in the world was the matter with her? She

didn't have sexual designs on this man. She wanted his name on a marriage certificate, that's all.

In name only.

For ninety days.

"Listen," he said, scooting out of the booth. "I need some time to think about this. I have other people to consider."

"I understand." A whole church full of people, she imagined. It took everything within her not to press him. Rightfully, he'd need time to digest all she'd told him, what she was asking of him.

She'd put a huge responsibility on his shoulders. With his decision, yes or no, he held Amy's and her mother's future in his hands.

"Where are you staying?" he asked.

Where *was* she staying? A wash of panic engulfed her. She hadn't fully considered all the angles. What had she expected? To breeze in, get married and move right in with him? This showed how little she'd indulged in rational thought lately. "The local motel, I guess."

"That's tricky. We've a hotel being built right now, but it's not open for business. I believe Mildred and Opal Bagley have a room available at the boardinghouse just up the street. I'll take you over there if you like, introduce you."

"No, I'll find it. You go ahead and do whatever it is you need to do."

He nodded and settled the tobacco-colored Stetson on his head, then gave the brim a tug in a quaint, polite gesture of goodbye. "I'll, uh, give you a call later, okay?"

"Sure." She wouldn't blame him if he went home, packed up his clothes and skipped town to find another church to head up. Far away from strange women who came to town waving a betrothal pact in his face.

DAN TILTED BACK in the leather chair in his study, listening to the ringing on the other end of the telephone. His mother would have admonished him for maltreating the furniture, but that was the thing about being alone. No one to please...or displease.

It was late afternoon on a Thursday, and the chances of catching his father at home were about the same as for Dan himself. It all depended on who was sick, who'd had a baby, if there was a special event that needed preparing for...

If a beautiful woman had proposed marriage.

Who'd have thought today would bring such a fork in the road of his life?

He gazed out the window where snow melted on the ground leading to the barn. His anticipated horseback ride would have to wait.

Because of Amy Marshall.

A name he'd never heard until two hours ago.

A woman whose life had inadvertently been entwined with his since before their births.

Oh, he firmly believed that all unions were written in the Big Book above. People were put in the right place at the right time for a reason. But to have his dad be the inadvertent instigator?

He was confused, a state he hadn't experienced in

a long time. Right warred with wrong, hormones with morals, improbability with sanity.

And at the center of that confusion was a woman who talked faster than a telemarketer trying to beat the dial tone.

She looked like a fashion model, dressed like a thrift-shop enthusiast and drove a four-wheel-drive Jeep. A mass of contradictions.

And that Deep Southern drawl...well, the combination of it all was messing with his libido, clouding his mind. He was actually starting to believe the proposition made perfect sense.

Was that his head, his heart or his body reacting?

His father spoke twice before Dan realized the telephone had finally been answered.

His feet dropped to the floor. "Dad. It's me."

"Dan. How's it going, son?"

"Good. Cold here. I bet you've got a pile of snow down there."

"More than our share. The fire's roaring, though, and the house is quiet. Your mother just brought in a tray of cocoa, and I'm indulging in an afternoon of reading."

"Preparing for Sunday's sermon?"

Phil Lucas laughed. "Actually no. I'm reading about a particularly gruesome monster in a Koontz novel. Scary stuff. The man's a brilliant writer."

Dan grinned. His father's love of horror and suspense novels didn't match his vocation or gentle character.

Which reminded him of his own confusion.

"I met someone today," Dan said. "Amy Marshall. The daughter of a friend of yours, Mark Marshall.''

''Ah, yes. How is Mark?''

''He died,'' Dan said gently. ''Quite some time ago.''

''Oh, I'm sorry to hear that.''

''So, the two of you didn't keep in contact?''

''Not since a few years after college. I moved to Montana and he stayed in Georgia.''

''Well, since you didn't stay abreast of each other, this is going to seem like an odd conversation.''

''How so?''

''When you were in college, did the two of you, uh, make some sort of crazy agreement?''

''No…wait a minute. Maybe. What's this about?''

Dan tilted his chair back again, tried to relay everything Amy had told him. His father listened without interrupting.

''I'd forgotten all about that marriage pact,'' Phil said at last. ''It was one of those things, you know? We never intended to see it through.''

''What made you write it down in the first place?''

''Emotion.'' Phil paused for a long moment. ''I've thought about Mark over the years, and I'm sorry he passed on without us getting in touch. I owed him more than that. Friendship. Especially since he saved my life.''

''What?''

''Yes, in college we were out ice fishing. The lake was frozen and I got cocky, went out farther than I should have. The ice broke and I went under. Mark took a big chance. If he hadn't come after me, I'd have died. But he saved me at great expense to himself. The ice could have given way beneath him, too. He didn't think, though—he just acted.''

Phil paused, and through the silence over the phone, Dan heard the sounds of material shifting against leather, the rattle of china clinking against wood.

''We were pretty shook up afterward, a couple of guys huddled by the fire trying to deny our emotions. We made a joke of it, slapped each other on the back, said we were bonded for life and shouldn't let the bond end with us, so we wrote it down. That was right before I started dating your mother.''

''But you lost contact.''

''Yes. Life often interrupts that way. People go their separate directions. I was grateful to him, though. If it had been anyone else, he might not have risked his life for mine. Mark was a bit of a daredevil, but he was a genuine man, also.''

So, if it hadn't been for Amy's father, Dan might never have been born. The pressure in his chest increased.

''Evidently Mark kept that paper the two of you wrote out.''

''I wonder why,'' Phil mused, then fell silent.

''Hard to say. But his father—Amy's grandfather— found it, and he filed it along with a codicil to his will.''

''It seems far-fetched. Are you worried that this woman has come to you with ulterior motives?''

''What motives? I'm not a rich man. I have nothing

to offer her—except my name for ninety days so her mother doesn't lose the family home.''

Phil remained silent. That wasn't what Dan was looking for. He'd figured he'd call his father and get immediate sage words of advice.

"What should I do, Dad?"

"I'm not the one you should be seeking answers from, son."

"I know. But I'm asking your opinion anyway."

"What is your heart telling you?"

"That she's a beautiful woman and she needs my help."

"Will helping her compromise your standing with your work?"

"No…at least I don't think so. It's more of a friendship proposal."

"You have to go by your own convictions, son."

"You're not giving me a whole lot of help, here."

"Like I said. I'm not the one whose help counts. What do you think of this Amy? Is she someone you can see yourself with twenty years from now?"

"I just met her, Dad. And I told you it would only be for three months. I…maybe it's the man in me talking."

"Evokes a few fantasies, does she?"

Dan laughed. Trust his dad to cut to the heart of the matter without pussyfooting around. "More than a few. It's more than that, though. There's a strong…I don't know what it is. Almost a rightness when I look at her. Besides that, she has a need. A genuine need—both she and her mother. And I'm the only one who can fill that need. If I don't, it's going to be rough on my conscience.''

"There's a lesson in everything that happens in our lives, you know that. Faith, Dan. That's your course. I can't advise you what to do. I will tell you that I'll support any decision you make. Your mother and I will stand behind you one hundred percent.''

Dan sighed. He was one of the lucky ones. Not every guy had family that offered unconditional love. "Thanks for the support. I need to talk to the church board before I make any firm decisions.''

"So you're considering accepting?''

"Yes. I'm considering.'' He couldn't believe it, but he was. He couldn't turn away someone in need.

A memory that he kept close at hand lest he be tempted to lose sight of who he was ran through his mind. After he'd gotten the drunk driving citation on the tractor, he'd known he needed to settle down. Judge Lester had gone easy on him, sentencing him to community service.

When his obligations were met, he'd gone back to college, determined to turn his life around and do what was right. To make his family proud. God knows, his reckless teenage years had given them enough sleepless nights.

Although his buddies were aware that he'd sworn off drinking, a bunch of guys had still tried to cajole him into attending a party off campus, laughing and promising not to lead him into sin but telling him that they needed a designated driver.

He'd declined, saying he had to study for an exam. That had only been a partial truth, an excuse really since he'd decided to clean up his act and avoid the party scene. At the time, he'd been full of his own righteousness, judging his friends by their actions.

Never mind that he'd been one of the biggest party hounds before that. He'd stood rigidly on his morals.

That night, tragedy had forever altered his rigidity. Alcohol, combined with rain-slick roads had resulted in a gruesome accident. One friend had died at the scene and another had ended up in a wheelchair.

The agony and guilt Dan had experienced was overwhelming.

He could have prevented the tragedy, but he'd turned his back on his friends. He'd been focused on what he thought was moral, instead of how he could help.

At the hospital, holding Chad's hand as his buddy wept over the loss of movement in his legs, Dan had made a vow never to make that mistake again.

To never turn his back on a person in need.

Now he was faced squarely with his own convictions. Amy and her mother needed his help. He could focus on the worry over desecrating sacred marriage vows, or he could trust his instincts and help a person who'd found herself backed into a corner with only one way out. A woman whose father had, without hesitation, risked his life for Dan's own father.

Amy wasn't asking him to engage in an illicit affair, wasn't advocating something that could be considered morally corrupt.

Just a ninety-day marriage. Three months of friendship and companionship.

That in itself was a difficult lure to resist. He gazed

around the study, a beautiful, warm room with rich oak paneling, complemented by wine and forest-green accents and hundreds of books on a multitude of subjects to keep him occupied and engaged.

But books, though comforting, didn't talk back.

It would be nice to have company.

A wife.

His stomach lurched at the thought.

He didn't know the purpose, or the "why" of finding himself in this position, but he'd learned over the years that there always was one. He had to trust that he was being led exactly where he was supposed to go for this particular time.

The next step, however, was the approval of the church board. If the door remained open, who was he to refuse to walk through it?

"I'll let you know what I decide, Dad."

Chapter Three

Amy looped the camera strap over her neck and made her way down the oak staircase at the Bagley widows' boardinghouse. Lavender sachets and potpourri scented the old white house, giving it an atmosphere that made it feel alive, as though the very air was a pair of loving arms waiting to envelop and welcome guests.

Aged furniture, hardwood floors, doilies on the back of the camel-hair sofa. It felt just like Grandma's house.

Everywhere she looked evoked a memory: reading *Black Velvet* in her grandmother's parlor and dreaming of grand adventures on horseback; drinking cocoa in the kitchen and poking the marshmallows beneath the surface of the chocolate, seeing how long they'd keep popping back up without melting; scattering jacks across a scuffed pine floor and wrestling the springy red ball away from the cat; ducking when Gramps stepped on one of the jacks that had skidded across the floor after a particularly zealous throw.

She'd had a wonderful childhood, and just now realized how much of it had been spent at her grand-parents' house. With Gramps.

A wave of sadness nearly buckled her knees. She loved that pigheaded, blustery old man and missed him with an ache that was like a raw, bloody wound.

What could he have been thinking to put her in this situation? In a strange yet magically beautiful town, asking a total stranger to share his roof and his name with her?

Shaking her head, she continued down the stairs and found the widows in what they fondly called their morning room. Although snow piled outside the door, the afternoon sun shone through the sheer lace curtains, bathing the aged woods with a soft buttery glow. Logs crackled in the fireplace, giving off the subtle scent of apple. A plate of oatmeal cookies and a china teapot rested on the coffee table.

Mildred and Opal both came to attention, as though they'd been waiting with their ears to the wall for her to come back down but were valiantly trying to act normal.

Amy saw right through them, and it made her smile.

"Did you get settled in, dear?" Mildred asked, laying aside her *National Enquirer* and ignoring Opal's censuring look at the magazine.

"Yes, thank you. The room is lovely."

"I remember, many years back, Dan came to stay with us for a spell. We put him up in the blue room you're in. Had a falling-out with his folks and ran away from home, didn't he, sister?"

Opal nodded and smiled, discreetly tucking Mildred's magazine beneath a pile of quilting books. "Ran right to us. We called Pastor Phil straight away, of course. Wouldn't want to interfere in a parent's business."

Amy imagined the sisters were attempting to open the door for her to give them more information on why she was here. But she was reluctant to do so.

Sure, if Dan accepted her offer, it would be public knowledge faster than a whirlwind could snuff a match. But until he gave her a decision, it was between the two of them. She owed it to him to guard his privacy.

All the widows knew was that she was here on personal business that had to do with Dan Lucas. They'd simply nodded and ushered her up to her room to get settled. But Amy knew they were itching to find out the details.

"At least, *I* didn't want to interfere," Opal amended. "Sister, on the other hand, was a menace."

"Just because I sided with the boy? Humph. You were always too rigid for your own good."

Amy was intrigued by the ladies' bickering. Love showed on their lined faces. Neither one cracked a smile, but the smile was clearly there, nonetheless.

She lifted her camera from where it hung at her chest, paused. "May I?"

Mildred fussed with her ash-blond pageboy cut. "Oh, I've eaten off my lipstick. I'm a mess."

"You're a vain old woman, is what you are," Opal said with a sniff.

Amy snapped a picture anyway, noticing the flashy polish on Mildred's fingernails. Siren-red with white polka dots. "What fun," she commented, nodding at Mildred's hands.

"Makes me dizzy," Opal complained. "I thought the Christmas tree decals she had Arletta paint on those fingernails was a mite gaudy and showy for the holidays, but they were better than this."

"It's a new year," Mildred defended, unfazed that her sister was maligning her manicure. "I needed a little whimsy."

"The butterflies you had last week weren't whimsy enough for you?" Opal demanded.

"Yes, well, they were difficult for Arletta."

"Why you can't have normal fingernails like the rest of us is beyond me."

"Never know when you'll attract a nice man. Doesn't hurt to be prepared. Men adore long fingernails and long hair." Mildred gave her hair another fluff and stared pointedly at Opal's military-short, steel-gray do.

"Men." Opal said the word dramatically. "It seems like that's all you can think about of late. Your Jerome, God rest his soul, would turn over in his grave if he knew you'd gone hormone crazy, like this."

"You're jealous because Lester Russo paid me a compliment at bingo Saturday night and didn't give you a second glance."

"Have you forgotten your Jerome and the judge came to fists over you back in forty-nine?"

"Yes, wasn't that romantic?" Mildred smiled and sighed like a dreamy girl after her first real kiss. Amy snapped the shot. Perhaps she'd send it to this Judge Lester person for Valentine's Day.

As the widows sniped and challenged each other, Amy's camera continued to whirl, her fingers automatically adjusting focus and angle as the shutter clicked away. A fond look; now exasperated; a sparkle of the eye; the barest hint of a suppressed smile— evidence that the bickering was a long-standing routine, a show.

She lowered the camera and grinned. "Did Arletta paint your whimsical butterflies freestyle, or use a decal?"

"Freehand. She's a bit of an artist. Understandable that a fingernail would be a difficult canvas, being so small and all. So we opted for the polka dots this week. Do you do portraits, dear?"

"Only for special friends. I predominantly do...I guess you'd say life portraits. Photographs that make a statement. Rare places and animals, also. I have an opportunity to work for *National Geographic*. They're sending me to Africa. If I do well, it could lead to other assignments and a steady position with the magazine."

"Oh, how delightful. You'll accept the offer, won't you?"

"Well..." A knock on the door saved her from answering.

Mildred rushed to answer it, fluttering her hands and commenting about the thrill of so much company on a Thursday afternoon.

"Dan! Land's sakes, boy. Were your ears burning?"

Booming laughter filled the front hall and carried to every corner of the room, transforming the atmosphere like static on a windy day. You couldn't see it, but you could feel it.

Amy's heart lurched. Good heavens, she'd asked this man to marry her. His height and his looks gave her a swift, instant punch, something she wasn't expecting. He wouldn't be an easy man, would want to call the shots rather than be manipulated.

She didn't know why she knew that. He was a minister. The title itself would make a person think of calm waters, even temperament. The turmoil he stirred inside her was anything but calm and even. Masculinity oozed from him in tangible waves.

And, darn it, he was still dressed like a cowboy. Brown Stetson, sheepskin-lined jacket, denim and flannel beneath that fit his body as though tailor-made to show off his physique. No baggy clothes to hide the goods.

Little wonder she'd had no clue to his identity. Was there a sin somewhere for a minister to sneak around like a normal man, just waiting to catch unsuspecting innocents like herself in a transgression? There ought to be rules, she decided, that mandated a clergyman should *look* like a clergyman.

Amy made herself calm down. She wanted to get on with things, find out if he'd made a decision. And at the same time, she wanted to put it off. This was a big step. A life-altering step.

Temporarily, she reminded herself.

"You talking about me again, Mildred?"

"You're a fine specimen of a man to talk about."

Opal sighed. "It soothes me to know that you've got an 'in' with the good Lord above. Otherwise, I'd be forced to accept that there's no hope for my sister. Honestly, speaking to a preacher in such a way. It's unheard-of."

"Well, now," Dan said. "I don't mind when a pretty woman comments on my manliness."

"See there," Mildred challenged, glaring at Opal. "Come in. Sister baked cookies and there's jasmine tea in the pot. We've cider, or cocoa if you'd prefer."

Dan looked past the sisters, and his gaze connected with Amy's. "Actually, I came to have a word with your houseguest."

"Boarder," Amy corrected automatically. She didn't know why she did it. Somehow, it seemed important to make the distinction. As though by paying for her room, she could control her destiny.

"Of course." He took off his hat and stepped toward her. "Miss Independent."

"And that's a bad thing?" She made herself stay where she was when every instinct inside her was urging her to step back. To flee. He brought in the crisp, clean scent of winter, and a powerful masculinity that stole her breath and made her heart trip like a finger stuck on a camera shutter.

Each time she saw him she wasn't prepared. For the zing. The physical beauty. And he *was* a beautiful man. His looks and virility made her forget who he was.

He stopped in front of her, grinned down at her. "Even independent people need to ask for help now and again."

Which was why they were both in this dilemma. "Your point."

He raised a brow, and she was struck once again at how he could pack such a powerful punch with a single gesture.

"Are we keeping score?"

Silence surrounded them. Amy realized the widows were uncharacteristically quiet, unabashedly eavesdropping.

She drew in a breath. "Would you like tea?"

Or me.

The thought popped into her head without so much as a by-your-leave and nearly shouted. She groaned. A lot was riding on whether he wanted her. Or at least would accept her presence in his life for the next three months.

Instead of continuing the volley that was clearly piquing the widows' interest, Dan turned to Mildred and Opal. "If you ladies don't mind, I'd like to steal your…boarder away for a bit. Give her a tour of the town."

"Oh, that's a lovely idea." Mildred's tone suggested just the opposite and Amy hid a smile. Clearly the sisters were hoping to get the scoop.

"What do you say, Amy?" Dan asked.

"Sure. Let me get my coat."

She raced up to her room and was back in a matter of minutes, carrying her backpack filled with extra camera bodies, lenses and film, a toothbrush and a change of socks and underwear.

They were standard items she carried as a matter of practice. She never knew when she'd get wet or stranded or whatever. Nothing worse than finding one's self unexpectedly in the middle of a great, career-making opportunity and have a camera or flash break, or blowing a shot because her feet were wet and cold.

The fact that she was stepping out with a minister, though, made the knowledge of carrying a toothbrush seem a little on the tawdry side.

Of course he didn't *know* she carried a toothbrush and underwear in her purse.

"Ready?"

Hoping her face wasn't glowing, since it certainly felt as though it was, she nodded and followed him to the porch. The only vehicle parked out front was her Jeep. Across the street at the sheriff's station, a beefy Bronco with a bar of emergency lights across its top straddled the diagonal line as though the driver had been more concerned with haste than parking courtesy.

She didn't imagine Dan had arrived in a county-issued sheriff's vehicle.

"Did you walk?"

"Yes. It's only a few blocks, and it's a nice day for it. Would you rather take your car?"

"Will I need it?" *Will I be coming back here?* Oh, there were so many things she didn't know. She had no idea how this was all supposed to work.

"Unless you're not up for a two-block walk, you won't need it. Most everything to see is right here along Main Street. You look in pretty good shape to me."

It caught her off guard that he was commenting on

her body. Especially when his eyes strayed to her derriere. Should he be doing that? She tugged at the hem of her coat, zipped it against the cold.

"Um, thank you. I try to stay in shape."

"Nice one, too."

He dropped the suggestive compliment into the conversation without so much as a hitch and started walking. Amy missed a step and had to jog to catch up with him.

"Do you always say things like that?"

"Compliments? Yes, when they're warranted. You have something against them?"

"No, but..."

He stopped so fast she plowed into him. He steadied her with hands at her elbows, looked down at her.

"But what, Amy?" His voice took on the barest hint of an edge. "I'm a minister, yes. That's my vocation. But I'm also a man. And that means I have the same urges, desires and thoughts as any other human being. So, let's clear the air right now and get it straight that *everything* on me or about me works the same as any other man's."

Well. I guess he told me how the cow eats the cabbage. Before she could think better of if, her eyes dipped to the front of his pants.

Oh, my. Tight jeans. Visual outline of the equipment.

She could have just died at the thought.

"Amy?"

"What?"

"Relax, okay?"

She sighed. They were standing in the middle of

the sidewalk on Main Street. A couple shopping at King's Western Wear had stopped to watch them. Brewer's Saloon was only a few paces farther. Her nerves were going to cause them to become a town spectacle.

He was right. He was just a man. With a capital *M*, to be sure, but a man nonetheless.

"Sorry. I don't know the rules."

"There aren't any. If you offend me personally, I'll let you know. Until then, just be yourself."

"Oh, now *there* you're leaving yourself wide-open."

He grinned and started them walking again. "Nothing wrong with a woman who speaks before thinking. You find out all kinds of interesting things that way."

She couldn't believe he was bringing up that unfortunate medical clinic incident. She choked, laughed. "You're no gentleman, Dan Lucas."

He winked at her. "I'm the epitome of a gentleman."

When it suited him, she imagined. "So, where are we going?"

"Unless you're truly interested in sight-seeing, I thought we'd go to my place."

Her heart lurched for no good reason, other than the idea of being alone with this man made her nervous. She was on pins and needles. She didn't know how to bring up the subject that was uppermost in her mind.

What if his answer was no? What if it was yes? This was so bizarre. She wished her grandfather was here. She'd like to look the man in the face and give him a piece of her mind. At the loudest decibel she could muster.

The two blocks down Main Street were long ones, nearly a half mile, she guessed. The street ended at a tee. To the left was Tillis's General Store and to the right was the medical clinic and veterinarian's office. Across the road was the small white church with gabled roof and a steeple atop, and next to it, the red brick courthouse, its flag waving in the wind as though sharing secrets with the spire above the steeple.

Dan led her around the back of the church, where a beautiful white Colonial-style two-story house stood, with a barn several yards beyond.

He paused. "Would you like to take a tour of the church first?"

"Maybe later."

"Then, why don't we start with the outside and work our way in?" he suggested, urging her with a hand at her back along the pathway to the barn.

She wondered if he was stalling, then decided he was probably trying to put her at ease. She appreciated his thoughtfulness. She felt like a fish flopping on the banks of a shallow riverbed, out of her element, wanting desperately to return to the safety of her own environment yet dependent on the benevolence of a passing bear to either have her for dinner, decide she wasn't worth the effort and leave her gasping, or to rescue her by throwing her back in.

Lord, she hated having to be rescued. That was her mother's MO. Not Amy's.

Off in the distance, a frozen creek bed snaked

across the land, outlined by naked cottonwoods. In the spring water would trickle over those rocks in a soothing litany of sound, and the terrain would come alive with budding hope as a new season promised change.

Amy wondered where her own life would be in the midst of that change.

The interior of the barn was a few degrees warmer than the brisk air outdoors. Wonderful smells of hay and leather surrounded her, with the more pungent scents of manure mixed in.

A gleaming chestnut horse poked its head over the half-door of the stall and nickered a welcome.

"How you doing, boy?" Dan called. Fondly he rubbed his hand over the horse's nose. "This is Moses. I promised him a ride today, but we didn't quite make it."

"Oh, now I feel bad." She joined Dan and lavished attention on the horse's silky coat. "It's my fault he had to stay cooped up in the barn."

Dan laughed. "Don't go feeling sorry for him. He gets plenty of exercise and is spoiled rotten by the kids from the reservation. Cheyenne Bodine, the sheriff, has the kids come out to his place for a day of riding at least once a month. I take Moses over there so he can get in on the fun. Plus, I have a young man who comes over to feed and exercise him. He doesn't lack for attention."

But Dan lacked for time, she surmised. He would continually set aside his own plans to accommodate others.

Like he had today. For her.

"Figures you'd give your horse a biblical name."

"Stereotyping, Amy?"

She had the grace to look chagrined, and he laughed and gave her hair a playful tug.

"He comes by the name rightly. He got caught in a flash flood in a riverbed and nearly died. It was quite a production getting him to safety."

"Like the Pharaoh's daughter fishing the baby out of the Nile."

"Yes—Moses." He grinned. "You paid attention in Sunday school."

She shrugged. "I was competitive. I wanted to be the first to fill up my page with merit stickers."

He laughed. "We might have to recruit you to teach Sunday school."

"Oh, I don't think I'm the type." Nor was she preacher's-wife material, either, but stranger things had been known to happen.

"So, do you have a church you attend regularly back home?"

It was a subtle probe, and she understood his reasoning. Still, she couldn't help but bristle a bit. "Is your decision pending on my spiritual beliefs?"

"No. But I'm planning to share my life with you in these next days to come and I'd like to know a bit more about you."

She didn't hear anything past the part about sharing his life with her. "You are?"

"Yes."

Tears filled her eyes. She didn't like it. Couldn't help it. She laid a hand on his chest, looked up at him. "Thank you."

The urge to run to the nearest phone and call her mother was enormous. But somehow it felt as though doing so would sully the sacrifice he was offering her, the selfless aid.

She didn't realize she'd been holding her breath. He was the answer to her problems, but at what expense to himself? This was what she wanted, what she desperately needed. But second thoughts intruded.

"Be very sure, Dan," she said softly. She didn't want to ruin this man's life or reputation. "Because I'm only agreeing to ninety days—a marriage in name only. That's it. We're clear on that, right? After that we're free to have the marriage annulled."

"Are you trying to talk me out of the decision?"

"No. I don't know. Maybe. I feel bad, but..." She looked up at him. "I need you."

"And I'm here for you."

She'd thought she'd feel a big burden lifted from her shoulders. It only got heavier.

He touched her cheek, made her look at him. "My eyes are wide-open, Amy. We'll help your mother keep her house."

"Thank you."

Moments passed while they looked at each other. She had no idea what he was thinking. She, however, was thinking that under any other circumstances, if he was any other man, she would have pressed her lips to his, perhaps even attempted to woo him into a relationship, to see where it would lead.

That would be in a perfect world. If they were both operating under their own free will.

"I hate this."

"What?"

"Being needy."

"Oh, stop it."

The order astonished her. She was getting maudlin. Nearly *whining*. Next to feeling helpless, whining was her number one pet peeve.

A smile started in her heart, reached her lips, turned into a laugh. "Bossy man."

"I can be."

"Well, I'm a stubborn sort. I'll let you get away with it this time, but in the future, you probably ought to know I won't sit still for it."

He laughed and tugged at her hair. "Duly noted."

"And to answer your earlier question, I was brought up in the Baptist church. We didn't attend regularly, but I've had the basic upbringing." Which made this whole marriage of convenience escapade difficult for her. Her worries were more for Dan than for herself, though. He didn't just talk the walk, he lived it. And she'd asked him to compromise it for her.

"What are we going to tell people?" she asked, thinking about the enormous impact this might well have on him.

"The truth always works best. I knew it might be embarrassing to tell everyone your business, but I felt it was important to level with the church board. I couldn't make this decision alone, and their approval was vital to my decision."

"And you got it?"

"Yes. You have to understand that Ozzie Peyton and his cohorts comprise most of the church board.

And with those four matchmakers, any sentence that starts with wedding has them rubbing their hands together and taking full credit for the romance. However, telling them something is like taking out a front-page ad in the newspaper. Word will spread anyway, so we might as well be up-front and get it out of the way."

"But you told your church people this wasn't about romance."

"That won't stop them from putting their own interpretation on it. Although I was a bit surprised that Ozzie admitted that he'd spoken with your grandfather a few months back."

"He did?"

"They were war buddies together—Ozzie hasn't lost contact with a single one of the men in his air squadron. He's a man whose loyalty runs deep, and I really admire that about him. When your grandfather began investigating the pact our fathers made and found out I was in Shotgun Ridge, he contacted Ozzie to inquire what kind of man I'd turned into."

Amy sighed. "I'm comforted that he at least did some homework, and didn't blithely try to tie me to a stranger who was an ax murderer or something."

"An ax murderer wouldn't dare live in Shotgun Ridge."

She rolled her eyes. "Still, when he found out you were a minister, I don't know why he didn't just drop the whole crazy thing."

"Ministers aren't priests. We do marry."

"But of your own free will. I wonder if Gramps had any idea what he was doing. It's so frustrating not being able to ask him. I want to be mad at him, but…"

"But you loved him."

"Yes. Cantankerous old goat. I can almost understand how he'd want to pull the strings in my life. But to involve you…"

"It's done, Amy. We can speculate all day and that's not going to give us the answers you're looking for. Or we can go forward. I opt for going forward."

"You're right."

"So what's on your agenda for the next few hours?" he asked.

Her heart raced. "You want to go get married right now?" *Well, duh, Amy. Isn't that what you're here for?*

"I was thinking more along the lines of going next door to the courthouse and getting the paperwork started. Even here, we've a bit of red tape to deal with."

"Oh. Of course. I wasn't thinking."

And she should have been. Because her ninety days were ticking away by the minute.

Chapter Four

They'd visited the courthouse and taken care of the preliminaries. The wedding was set for Saturday at eleven o'clock.

Now that the wheels were firmly in motion, Amy's nerves were even more of a mess. She was doing this for her mother, she reminded herself. But the very idea of marriage—especially to a minister who was firmly entrenched in this town—made her want to hyperventilate.

She wanted nothing more than to go back to the boardinghouse and hide under the covers for a while, but Dan had other plans.

"It's Thursday night dinner at Brewer's. Nobody cooks on Thursday night. I know we just had lunch there, but this is one of those be-there-or-be-square sort of things. Plus it'll be the perfect opportunity for us to announce the engagement."

Her heart rate went straight through the roof. Nobody had said anything about making public announcements. Though how she'd ever imagined they were going to hide a marriage for three months was beyond her. Dan had told her they should tell the truth. She'd figured that would be on a case-by-case basis.

"I don't have a problem with being square."

He laughed and draped her coat around her shoulders. "Well, I do. I have a reputation to uphold around here."

She nearly groaned. "Are you sure I'm not fixing to ruin it for you?"

"I think you'll be pleasantly surprised by the people of this town."

BREWER'S AND SHOTGUN RIDGE in full swing were nothing like she'd expected. It seemed as though folks had come out of the woodwork.

Every time she turned around or took two steps, it required an introduction—Hannah and Wyatt Malone, Dora and Ethan Callahan, Emily and Cheyenne Bodine, Chance and Kelly Hammond. She didn't even try to keep all the children straight or remember who belonged to whom. Everybody seemed to be holding somebody else's child, and it was simply too confusing for her first day here.

To tell the truth, she was a bit overwhelmed by all the names and faces she'd be expected to remember. Although she was from a midsize town in Georgia, where some of the small-town dynamics prevailed, the Marshall name had set her apart, thrust her into a different social circle. The upper-class, country-club folks.

Admittedly, she'd been the rebel amongst their midst, not buying into the polite smiles when she knew they were judging the inappropriateness of her clothing or her nonconformist ways.

Gramps had money, and it was a well-guarded secret that Amy and her mother weren't in the same income class, that her mother, at least, was dependent on the goodwill of Ben Marshall.

But Chandra Marshall was the perfect Southern lady and a big advocate of keeping up appearances. Amy had been surprised that she'd hadn't pitched a fit when Amy had taken the waitress job at the gentleman's club.

Kelly Hammond, the doctor's wife and also a doctor herself, placed a hand on Amy's arm and studied her face.

"Dan told us you'd been in the clinic earlier, but decided not to wait. How are you feeling now?"

Amy's gaze whipped to Dan's. *You told them?* It was a silent question, but he picked up on it as though she'd spoken aloud.

He laughed, and teased, "Shame on you. I only mentioned the part about the dizzy spell."

She sucked in a breath, nearly whacked him before she thought better of it. The man had the very devil in his eyes. Although she knew he'd never betray a confidence, she also knew she'd have to stay on her toes around this guy.

Turning back to Kelly, she said, "Low blood sugar, I'm sure. I hadn't eaten and scared myself. It was only a little vertigo."

"You might want to come in and let Chance or me check you over, maybe do a blood workup."

"No. I'm fine now."

"Okay. But if you need us, we're here for you."

The genuine words touched Amy. They were words she heard often during the evening. Probably due to the fact that each person asked the sixty-four-thousand-dollar question—"What brings you to Shotgun Ridge?"

With Dan sticking close by her side, raising eyebrows in the bargain, he easily elevated her flustered nerves. In his charmingly teasing manner, he forestalled probing questions, informing everyone that he was going to save Amy's vocal cords by waiting until everyone arrived, at which time he'd make a blanket introduction.

The curiosity and speculation in the room was palpable, but acceptance and patience went right along with it.

Before long, Amy felt herself relax enough to give Dan a gentle nudge. "I can see you're itching to mingle. I'll be fine on my own. Go."

"Are you trying to get rid of me?"

"Yes. You make me nervous."

The gleam in his eye was very unpreacherlike. "And you're making me the most envied guy in the room."

"Get out." She still wore hiking boots, jeans and a man's flannel shirt. Hardly the attire of a lust-inspiring woman. Besides, every man in this room had eyes only for his own wife. She'd already learned that the majority of them were newlyweds.

As the evening geared up with a community spirit that continued to awe Amy, they munched on pretzels and chips, laughed, played pool…and Dan smoked cigars. Even Dora Callahan partook as her husband watched on indulgently.

Dan had already mentioned the indulgence to her, but seeing it made him even more of a confusion in her mind.

Why wouldn't the man stay in the pigeonhole she kept trying to fit him in?

Latecomers straggled in, and the noise level in the room increased, country music vying with laughter and happy shrieks of children. There was one waitress, Maedean, as well as Iris Brewer to handle all the customers.

When Amy overheard Maedean explaining that their other waitress had called in sick with the flu, she excused herself from the hot and heavy pool game taking place between Chance Hammond and Cheyenne Bodine.

She admired Iris Brewer. The woman was small in stature but worked harder than three people twice her size. Amy couldn't imagine her own mother taking so much initiative, taking it all in her stride with a laugh here and a touch there.

Slipping behind the bar, she gave Iris a wink. "You'll wear yourself to a frazzle. I'll take care of the drinks, you just bring me the orders."

"Oh, you're a guest. I can't let you work."

"My grandmother always said many hands make light work." She glanced out at the overflowing diner. "In this case, at least lighter. It's getting so crowded in here, pretty soon I'll have to go outside to change my mind."

Iris chuckled. "That it is. Thursday night tradition

at Brewer's is like church on Sundays. You miss it and somebody will be wanting to know why. Still, I hate to toss you into the fire this way."

"Shoo. I've got plenty of snap in my garters and can pour a beer on tap with the best of them." Plus, she needed a distraction. The knowledge that Dan intended to announce their coming marriage kept her in a constant state of apprehension. "I'm like a chameleon. I adapt well to my surroundings."

At a silent nod from her husband, Lloyd, Iris accepted Amy's offer.

"Bless you, hon—oh, Eden and Stony are here at last. I was beginning to worry. I should at least stay and introduce you."

A woman holding a chubby baby wrapped in a fluffy pink blanket came in, flanked by an incredibly tall cowboy gently gripping the hand of an energetic, pixy of a girl around six.

"Go," Amy coached. "I can do my own introducing. As you can see, I'm not exactly the shy type."

Iris gave her a quick hug. "I think I'm going to like you, Amy Marshall." And with that, she rushed off to feed the hungry, leaving Amy a little stunned by the spontaneous show of affection.

Eden took one look at Amy behind the bar and headed straight over. "Hey, there. I'm Eden Stratton. The tall, silent guy here, is my husband, Stony."

"Amy Marshall."

"Lord have mercy, y'all are hoppin' tonight. Who ordered a population explosion when I wasn't looking?"

A fellow Southerner, Amy thought. She didn't

know why, but for some reason that made her feel more at home.

"I was told you either had to be here or you're out of the loop. I guess folks take that kind of serious."

Eden laughed and handed the baby in her arms to her husband. "That they do. Go talk boy stuff, Stony. I'll just slip in here and make myself useful."

The child was nearly swallowed up in the tall cowboy's arms. He smiled indulgently at his wife, yet cautioned, "Don't overdo."

A special look passed between husband and wife. "Don't fuss, now."

Shaking his head, he pressed a kiss to her temple and went off to join friends.

Amy stared. What would it be like to have a man be so devoted to her? To love her so deeply the whole world could see it?

She shook away the thought. She wasn't looking for love. She had a career waiting for her.

"How old's the baby?"

"Five months. Sarah's a joy. She does, however, cause us to be unforgivably late on occasion." Eden snagged an apron from behind the bar.

"Are you a waitress, then?" Amy asked.

"A caterer by trade, actually. I'm in charge of the dessert menu here. But I'm happy to pitch in when Iris gets swamped. The woman would sooner eat a bug than ask for help."

"I heard that," Iris said, bustling back to the bar with a list of orders. "Eden Stratton, you're in no condition to be working."

"Would everyone quit fussing?" She turned to

Amy. "Sarah's my miracle baby. I wasn't sure I'd even get the chance to have her. Now we've just found out I'm expecting again. What everyone around here doesn't seem to realize is that it's when I'm *not* pregnant that they should worry. A little problem with anemia and such. When I'm in the family way, I blossom."

"Well, you should be blossoming at the table with your husband," Iris admonished. "Did you meet Amy? She came with Dan. And before you ask any questions, Dan's already warned us off. Some mysterious thing he intends to tell the lot of us about. I've a mind to pump her for information, but my manners won't let me."

"Mine will." Eden tied on the apron, her smile letting Amy know that she was just kidding. That she respected whatever boundaries had been set.

"Shame, shame," Dan said from behind them. "There's nothing secret going on. You know how I like to stand up in front of folks and sermonize. Amy's simply indulging my need to play to an audience."

"The man's so modest," Eden said, going up on tiptoe to press a kiss to Dan's cheek. "However, he does have a gift for gab and showmanship."

Amy felt a little out of place. These people knew Dan, had grown up with him most likely. And here she was, fixing to become his wife. And she didn't know a thing about him.

Dan slipped behind the bar and moved next to Amy. When he'd looked up and seen her gone from the table, he'd had a queer feeling in the pit of his stomach, a moment of panic that she'd skipped town as suddenly as she'd breezed into it. The jolt of emotion puzzled him, but he left it alone.

"It appears to be getting more crowded behind this bar than out on the floor," Amy said, even though Eden and Iris had bustled away and it was only the two of them left. "Would you go sit down and make it easier on your waitress? It's tough when she takes your order and you won't stay in one place."

"Speaking from the voice of experience?"

"As a matter of fact, yes." She gave him a look that made him sweat, made his mind conjure images of what she'd look like wearing a skimpy waitress outfit. An outfit appropriate for a gentleman's club.

Oh, man.

He cleared his throat. "I thought I'd better make sure you understood the meal was on me. Didn't want you thinking you had to work for your supper if your funds were low."

"My funds are fine. Iris needed the help and I happen to be fairly adept at serving."

"Dressed a bit differently, I'm sure." *Oh, brother.* He hadn't meant to voice that teasing thought. Why had he, he wondered when he saw her eyes widen.

Maybe because he had so much admiration going on inside, he wasn't sure what to do with it. Not many women would come to a town and blend in and help out when they hardly knew anyone's name. "You're a good person, Amy."

She shrugged.

"No, I mean it. You saw that Iris needed a hand and you lent it without hesitation."

She busied herself loading a tray with drink orders, and he noted that her hands were trembling slightly.

"She reminds me of my grandmother." Sadness tinged her voice and something more, something he couldn't identify. Yearning? A need to belong?

He stared at her for another minute, then grabbed the tray filled with sodas and a couple mugs of beer. He had the next three months to find out what made Amy Marshall tick. Right now, he could tell she was holding on by a thread and doing her darnedest to appear otherwise. "Which table do these go to?"

"Horning in on my tips, Preacher?"

"Now that you mention it, that's a great idea. I'll add it to the church collection plate and folks won't even know they've given twice."

"Oh, now you've done it. How can I begrudge the church money in favor of my traveling fund?"

Her smile was devilish, but he knew good and well she wasn't helping out for monetary gain. There was a sweetness about her. A need to please others that he'd be willing to bet warred with her need to please herself.

He couldn't pinpoint why this woman intrigued him so much. But she did.

And that Southern drawl, the way she put an extra syllable to nearly every word, made him want to keep her talking just so he could hear it.

Before he made a fool out of himself, he hoisted the drink tray, balanced it on one palm and set out across the room to do a little showing off, laughing out loud in anticipation of the good-natured teasing he'd no doubt get.

He should have been an entertainer, he thought with another laugh.

AMY ATE HER SECOND hamburger of the day, her nerves so raw she'd likely be up all night with indigestion. Long tables had been set up in the back as though Dan and his neighbors had requested a private banquet.

This was a very close-knit group, she realized. Children raced around like frolicking rabbits, happily outrunning an imaginary fox. Babies fussed and were soothed by the closest set of arms—usually male. The sight touched Amy's heart.

When everyone had finished their meal, Dan, sitting beside her, squeezed her hand. "Ready?"

Caught off guard, adrenaline shot straight to her head. He was about to make the announcement. "Now?"

"Have pity on my neighbors. We've made them so curious, they're about to burst but are too polite to say so. Do you want to stand up with me?"

"No!"

He squeezed her hand again and scooted his chair back.

Amy couldn't breathe. Suddenly, desperately, she wanted out of here. Why hadn't she left earlier? Pleaded exhaustion, let him deal with this on his own so she wouldn't have to be in the spotlight, search for censure in the faces around her?

But that was cowardly. And the reaction of these people was important. If Dan was going to run into opposition, she needed to know, to stand by him as he'd agreed to do for her.

"Okay, everyone. Listen up."

The sudden silence in the room was nearly comical, evidence that they'd all been waiting with bated breath for this moment.

Dan grinned. "Never say I don't know how to work a crowd."

Groans and comments about his head swelling too big to fit beneath his Stetson were bandied about. Caught up in the moment, Amy felt her nerves abating.

The exclusive look Dan aimed down at her told her he was attempting to do just that. That if she put herself in his hands she'd be fine; he'd be strong enough for the both of them.

A giddy feeling of excitement stirred in her stomach. This was a take-charge man. Strength radiated from him. He'd be the kind of ally a person would want covering their back.

Why did she keep getting those feelings of needing him, depending on him, when she was a woman who prided herself on not needing or depending on anyone but herself?

"You've all met Amy Marshall by now, and you're itching to know why she's here—not that a person can't just come to our fine town for no other reason than that we're a great group of people."

Everyone chuckled and glanced at Ozzie Peyton and his pals.

"You're all friends. I've talked this over with the church board, and for once, Ozzie, I'm glad to see you boys could mind your tongues and not upstage me on the news. Amy and I are going to be married this Saturday.''

The murmurs among his friends were congratulatory rather than judgmental. Still Amy felt a rush of heat to her face.

''I know it all seems very sudden—and it is. So, let me tell you a story about sacrifice and selflessness,'' he began.

Amy's nails bit into her palm as she squeezed her fists in her lap, heart pounding. But as words poured out of him, she forgot all about her nerves.

She'd thought she'd feel conspicuous. Instead, as Dan told the story of their fathers fishing together— Amy's father saving a life despite the danger to his own, the emotions they must have been feeling, the pact they'd made—she listened, caught up in the story, even forgetting that it was *her* father he spoke about.

He knew how to hold an audience, knew how to paint a picture with words, evoke an emotion. By the time he got to the terms of the will, there didn't appear to be a person in the room who wasn't ready to march them right over to the courthouse to make sure Amy's mother didn't lose the family home.

Acceptance.

When he finished, he drew her up to stand beside him, casually looping his arm around her shoulders. Amy thought this might be a bit much, given the circumstance, but she didn't pull away.

Neighbors and friends gathered around to offer congratulations.

A striking woman, who Amy had been dying to meet but hadn't gotten the opportunity to yet, stepped up and took Amy's hand.

"That was a moving story. Even more so for those of us who lived here in the days Phil Lucas was pastor of the church. We've not met, but I'm Judith Hammond. Chance Hammond, that good-looking doctor over there, is my son."

"I'm so glad to meet you," Amy said. "I know and admire your work."

"Thank you, dear." Judith graciously accepted the compliment but didn't make a big deal. One would never know this woman was a famous artist. Like the rest of the crowd, she was totally genuine.

"My husband and I extended our vacation well past the New Year. We came to attend our son's wedding and to get to know our new daughter-in-law and granddaughters. Heaven knows, we tried to convince Chance and Kelly to take advantage of us and scoot off on a honeymoon, but they're worried about the health of the community, and the best we could do was entertain and spoil the children, Jessica and little Kimberly." She gazed lovingly at Chance and Kelly.

"This is tacky, I admit, but what I'm leading up to is that I adore weddings. And two of them in a matter of weeks is too delicious to resist. Would it be awfully presumptuous of us to attend?"

Amy didn't know what to say. She knew Judith Hammond by reputation. The woman painted wonderfully whimsical fairies, had her own art gallery in Helena. It would be like having a celebrity at her wedding. She recalled that Judith was originally from

Shotgun Ridge. And being such a close-knit community, it was natural to expect that you'd have a standing, open invitation to all the important goings-on.

Like a wedding between the preacher and a cocktail waitress—albeit a waitress who aspired to have as recognizable a name in the arts as Judith Hammond did.

But this wasn't a real wedding. It should be a small affair and not involve the entire town.

She looked at Dan for guidance, but good Southern manners had her saying, "Of course you're invited. We're scheduled for eleven o'clock at the court-house."

"Not the church?" Judith glanced at Dan, who shrugged.

"It seemed easier," Amy said quickly. "Since Dan can't very well perform his own ceremony."

Amy had been adamant on that point, though. Somehow, it made it less…immoral by marrying at the courthouse instead of the church. Maybe less *real* was what she was thinking. Less of a moral dilemma for Dan. Although, she had to admit that she was actually the one creating mounds of guilt over what they were doing. Dan seemed to simply roll with the punches.

She hadn't counted on the masses to want to show up as witnesses, though. My gosh, she hadn't even invited her own mother, yet everybody *else's* mother planned to be there.

She and Dan had agreed that since time was of the essence, it wouldn't be fair to encourage their families to drop what they were doing and rush to town. Dan's mother was committed to teach Sunday school, his father had a sermon to preach in his own church on Sunday, and Amy's mother…well, getting Chandra from one place to the next on her own would be a challenge. Amy didn't think her mother had ever made airline reservations or traveled by herself on vacation.

So they would go on without them. A simple ceremony to fulfill the terms of the will.

How in the world had this whole fiasco mushroomed into such an event?

And why didn't anybody think to bat an eye or raise an objection?

Chapter Five

With her belongings once again packed in her Jeep, Amy arrived at the courthouse a little before eleven and promptly hid out in the rest room.

Not that she was worried about any of the silly bad-luck superstitions over seeing the groom before the ceremony.

Honestly, she was marrying the *preacher*. He probably didn't even believe in superstitions.

Oh, Lord. Every time she thought about what she was fixing to do, nausea roiled in her stomach like waking up with a hangover to the smell of breakfast cooking.

She smoothed a hand over her stomach and checked her reflection in the mirror. Since she'd set out on a mission she'd prayed would end in marriage, she'd packed a simple dress in anticipation of the ceremony.

The powder-blue sheath had a fine silk mesh overlay that gave respectability to the low-cut bustline, stretching over the crepe in a mock-turtleneck style with close-fitting sleeves. The hem ended about an inch above her knees, which was perfectly respectable, she told herself. Everything else in her closet that was halfway dressy and suitable for winter had seemed inappropriate. The red wool was too racy. The basic black too somber. The khaki too drab.

But was this okay?

Oh, damn it, she looked like a robin's egg wrapped in the backyard hammock.

Maybe she was making too much of this. Maybe she should have just worn a pair of slacks and a nice sweater. She was on her way to the car, intending to tear through her suitcases and find a change of clothing when Ozzie intercepted her.

"Well, now, you're lookin' pretty as a breath of spring, you bet."

Her heart was pounding in her chest. "Are you sure? It's not too much?" *Given the circumstances.*

Ozzie drew her arm into the crook of his elbow in a fatherly gesture and patted her hand. "Now, don't go gettin' all fussy on me. Why, my Vanessa used to change clothes three times before she'd settle on a church dress that suited her mood. Always did end up wearing the one she'd had on in the first place, you bet. Goes to show you should pay attention to your instincts and be done with it."

Amy sighed. "If I paid attention to my instincts, I'd be in my Jeep and halfway through Wyoming by now."

Ozzie gazed down at her, his vivid blue eyes filled with compassion. "You never know what the good Lord has in mind when we find ourselves in the middle of a scary new venture, but over all my years of livin'—I'm not sayin' how many, mind you—I've figured out it's best to go along and not question.''

"Gramps didn't have the right to involve Dan this way. He was disappointed in me and wanted me to do something different with my life.''

"Now that's just not so. I spoke to Ben Marshall not two months ago, and all he talked about was you. He was proud as punch, you bet. So, you get that thought out of your head, you hear?''

Tears backed up in her throat and she nodded.

Ozzie patted her hand, looked away, typically a man uncomfortable with a woman about to start squalling all over him.

"I came lookin' for you to ask a favor,'' Ozzie said.

"Of me?''

"Yep. For all those months we spent together in the war, Ben and me were like family. Since he's not here to do the honors himself, I wondered if you'd let me be his stand-in and give you away.''

Now the tears that had been stuck in her throat worked their way to her eyes. "Oh, damn, my mascara's gonna run down my face and I'll look like a circus clown,'' she murmured, then clapped her free hand over her mouth.

Ozzie cackled. "We're in the courthouse. Cursin' is allowed. Besides, that accent of yours just plum tickles me. Makes the words sound perfectly polite and respectable, you bet.''

Amy repeated the word in her mind as Ozzie dabbed at her cheeks with his white handkerchief. *Day-am.* Didn't sound so respectable to her. She was used to hearing herself talk, never considered that she had an accent, just that everyone else sounded different.

"So, what do you say, Miss Amy?" He put the handkerchief back in the pocket of his western-cut suit jacket. "Will you do me the honor of letting me walk you down the aisle?"

She sighed, touched beyond words, actually glad to have his support. Her knees were shaking like mad.

"It would be *my* honor, kind sir. Though I imagine we'll have to pretend on the aisle since we're just going before the judge."

"Ah, now. I see you've not yet taken into consideration the determination of this here town. Why the ladies can plan a wedding faster than a cowboy can rope a steer. There'll be an aisle."

He led her toward the room the judge had designated to perform weddings in, but her steps slowed at the last minute.

Ozzie looked at her patiently, waiting for whatever she had to say.

"Are you sure this isn't going to hurt Dan? The fact that I'm going in there with the express purpose of obtaining a piece of paper and only planning to stay for the required three months? I'm embarrassed that the whole town knows I've got one foot out the door before I've even stepped all the way in."

Ozzie patted her hand again. "My Vanessa always said folks shouldn't place too much store on what everybody else thinks, and just concentrate on their own selves. She was a right smart lady, the schoolteacher here. Made it a point to teach every one of the younguns that same lesson. You just put those worries out of your mind now. Your heart's in the right place. That's what's important.''

She squeezed Ozzie's arm, kissed his cheek. ''Thank you, Ozzie. I can see why Gramps called you 'friend.'''

OUTWARDLY, DAN WAS CALM. Inwardly he was a mess. He was the one who usually officiated at weddings. He'd even performed a couple at the courthouse.

He understood why Amy wanted it here rather than at the church, though. She was thinking about him. Wanting to take as much focus off what she perceived as the morality issues as possible. So were the vows any less sacred in a courthouse than in a church?

Not likely. But she'd been adamant. How could he ignore the pleading in her misty green eyes, the earnestness in that soft Southern drawl?

He looked around at all of his friends who'd gathered to witness the occasion, to lend their friendship and support and give their blessings—regardless of the circumstances or the outcome.

Where before this had been a town filled with bachelors and very few women and children, now the balance had shifted. Most of his buddies were married and settled into family life. Dan had performed the services himself.

Something was in the air—granted the four town meddlers had dipped their fingers in, giving a nudge. Ozzie Peyton and company. Dan nearly laughed out loud.

The old guys were rubbing their hands together, he could tell. They claimed that they were led by God above. Funny how God hadn't mentioned anything to Dan himself over intentions to subtly maneuver the town's men into marriage, but Dan hadn't figured it was his business to butt in with what the geezers were continually plotting.

"Show time," he murmured when Lester Russo came into the room, wearing the black robe that marked his profession.

When Dan was nineteen, he'd stood before this man and been sentenced to three months of community service.

Now that same man was going to perform his marriage ceremony.

He noticed the familiar way the judge was bending close to speak to Mildred Bagley. He'd had an inkling that the two had been keeping company lately. Now *there* was an explosive combination.

The judge patted Mildred's shoulder and she trilled with laughter. Smiling, his step springier than normal, he moved to take his place in front of Dan.

"About time I get to perform a marriage in my own chambers. I was put out with you when you hogged in on the Stratton and the Bodine unions. I'm still a little put out that you didn't let me do this over at your church. Since you've usurped my place here several times, I was looking forward to encroaching on your territory."

Dan laughed. "I guess I hadn't realized we were in competition."

"Of course, we're in competition. And it's not nice

to one-up your elders. However, I'm feeling somewhat mollified by today's events. Here, now, isn't that
a lovely sight."

Dan turned and saw Amy on Ozzie's arm. His heart
stuttered. She met his gaze, held it for a charged moment, a moment that caused the room to recede, to
encompass only the two of them.

Then a distressed look came over her face, and she
whispered something to Ozzie, let go of his arm and
bolted from the room.

His heart sank to his stomach, but before he could
go after her, Ozzie shook his head, and Dan checked
the impulse.

She was back in a moment, handing a camera to
Ozzie. He should have known. She rarely took two
steps without her prized Nikon. For some reason, that
simple act of consistency calmed him, made him
wonder why he'd felt so bereft when it appeared she'd
changed her mind.

Soft music filled the room, amplified from a portable stereo that had more buttons and gadgets than
the control panel of a 747 jet. Ethan Callahan's, he
noted. Figures. Those Callahan guys owned more
fancy sound equipment and big-boy toys than anyone.

When Amy drew next to him, he reached for her
hand. It was ice-cold and trembling. He smiled, pulled
her close.

"Relax," he whispered. "It'll be fine."

"Who gives this woman in marriage?" the judge
asked.

"I believe that'd be my honor," Ozzie said. "As

mayor of this here town and friend of Ben Marshall, you bet.''

The judge glared, cleared his throat. ''A simple 'I do' would have been sufficient.''

''Didn't want to upstage the bride and groom's line,'' Ozzie countered, eyes twinkling.

''Sit down, Peyton,'' the judge ordered, clearly intending to show who was in control in his courtroom.

Amy, who was such a wreck she feared she'd throw up, looked from the judge to Ozzie. The morning was going from bizarre to outright crazy. The judge and mayor fussing like two old crows over the same worm. Honestly.

When she saw the obviously tickled smile on Dan's face, her own smile grew. ''Are they always like this?''

''Always. Seems to have gotten worse since Lester's been keeping company with Mildred.''

''Can I please have some order and respect in my court?'' Judge Russo demanded.

Amy snapped to attention. Everything would be all right, she thought. The unorthodox bickering and talking insured that this wouldn't be a traditional ceremony. And that knowledge was just what she needed to calm her nerves.

''Yes, sir. I apologize for speaking out of turn.''

Dan lifted a brow, and the judge, mollified, nodded and proceeded.

Aware of the circumstances, or coached beforehand by Dan, the judge didn't sermonize, but got right down to business.

In a daze, by rote, Amy spoke when she was

prompted and didn't dwell on the words, didn't allow herself to consider the sacred promises. They were simply a means to an end. In fact, the judge nearly rushed them through the ''I do's.''

Then came the flair of dramatics. With a snap, he closed the book.

''By the power granted to me by the state of Montana, I pronounce you husband and wife. Dan, you have my express permission to kiss your bride.''

Amy's eyes widened. *Oh, no.* She hadn't considered this part.

Dan's smile was slow and one hundred percent male. ''It's customary.''

Her palms went damp and her heart thudded. He slid his hands up her neck, his fingers spearing gently through her hair, and drew her face ever so slowly to his.

It was a seduction. Pure and simple. Right here in the courthouse with the whole town looking on. He gazed at her as though she'd hung the moon and stars, as though this was real…as though she were the love of his life.

With his eyes open, he made sure he had her complete attention, held it for a long, humming moment, then slowly lowered his head until his lips touched hers.

She expected him to just give her a brief peck.

Instead he pulled her into the kiss and lingered. Oh, how he lingered. His skin was freshly shaven and smooth, his lips soft and masculine. A hint of cologne filled her nostrils, a combination of citrus and sandalwood.

Their bodies weren't touching. Just their lips. He held her in place with only his hands gently cradling her face. And with his mouth.

Her first thought was *What can he be thinking?* After that, she ceased to think. Her eyes closed, blotting out the room, the people, the reason they were here. Nothing existed except the two of them and this kiss.

And, oh, what a kiss. His mouth opened slightly over hers, yet he didn't use his tongue, didn't push for carnality or make her jaw ache trying to adjust to the fit.

The fit was perfect.

Sensuality radiated in waves, but uppermost was romance.

This was the most romantic meeting of lips she'd ever encountered. She'd seen photographs that depicted what she was feeling at this very moment, but she'd never actually experienced it.

When he lifted his head, she knew her expression was stunned. The whole thing couldn't have lasted longer than a slow count of five, but it was the longest, most exquisitely life altering count of five she'd ever imagined.

The sound of clapping snapped her back to the present. Dazed, she turned to her new neighbors and friends and smiled, tried to cover the turmoil inside her.

For the life of her, she couldn't come up with a single word to speak to her husband. So she stepped away from him, glad when his friends moved in to shake his hand, avert his attention, glad when the ladies circled her like excited sorority sisters who'd just found out she'd been pinned by the star quarterback.

In this case, the town minister.

Oh, my gosh, what had she gotten herself into? What had Gramps gotten her into?

And where in the world had Dan Lucas learned to kiss like *that?*

TWO HOURS LATER, Dan and Amy politely made their escape. She slid into the driver's seat of the Jeep and raised a brow at Dan, who was checking out the windows and grinning like a fool.

"Are you getting in or not?"

He shrugged and opened the passenger door. "Guess it wouldn't look too good if we split up so soon."

She closed her eyes, reminded again that this wasn't real. She'd been feeling out of sorts ever since that kiss. As though he were a true husband and this was a love match, Dan hadn't left her side during the reception that had followed.

The ladies had prepared a potluck worthy of a five-star dinner party, complete with a wedding cake baked and decorated by Eden Stratton. Dora Callahan had appropriated Amy's camera from Ozzie and snapped enough photos to fill two albums.

Amy could still taste the butter cream frosting on her lips. And the taste of that incredible ceremonial kiss.

Although she only had to move her Jeep five hundred yards, from the courtyard parking lot to the rectory behind the church, some romantic soul had scrawled "Just Married" on her back window and tied a set of cowbells to the bumper that made an attention-drawing racket.

Dan took it in stride.

Amy felt conspicuous.

She shut off the Jeep's engine in front of the Colonial-style two-story house, vowing to get rid of those annoying cowbells and take a bucket of soapy water and sponge to erase the shoe-polish words.

The sooner things got back to normal—or as normal as could be expected—the better.

She hoisted a suitcase out of the back and Dan grabbed a cumbersome crate, his muscles straining, testing the seams of his suit jacket. He might have looked like a powerful businessman except for the Stetson on his head and the pointy-toed boots on his feet.

"Man alive, what's in here?"

"Film-processing equipment."

"Heavy stuff."

The conversation felt stilted. She didn't know how to act, was jumpy as a cat as she preceded him into the house.

This wasn't a traditional wedding day, so there would be no wedding night.

Which made that mind-blowing kiss at the altar even more confusing. Darn it, she had to stop thinking about that—*obsessing* on it.

"Where should I put my things?"

"There're six bedrooms. Choose any one you want."

"Except yours." Cryin' all night. Why had she said that? She didn't know where to look, certainly didn't want to meet his eyes. The man saw too much, would likely read her mind—which had taken on a will of its own and was wallowing in areas it had no earthly business wallowing in.

Dan set down the box. "Here, let me help you with that suitcase."

She tightened her hold on the handles. "I'm fine. I can take it from here." It was a petty stand to make, but she did it anyway. She'd given up so much already, relied on him too much.

He shoved his hands into his pockets, evidently feeling as uncomfortable as she was.

"How do you want to work this?"

He was talking about the tension between them born of the knowledge that they'd be living in close quarters for the next three months. That had been one of the stipulations in the will.

Amy shrugged. "Like roommates, I guess."

"Roommates," he repeated, his expression bland, unreadable. "All right. I've got a sermon to prepare. If you need me, I'll be in the study."

If you need me.

That was the problem. She didn't *want* to need him.

Not knowing what else to do, Amy lugged her suitcase up the wide oak staircase, peering into rooms as she passed.

The bedrooms were all furnished, the house large and welcoming with its warm-toned woods and homemade quilts. She chose a room decorated in soothing hues of cream and ivory, telling herself the decor appealed to her senses, not the fact that it was directly across the hall from the master suite—Dan's room.

She ran her hand over the down comforter and flannel case covering the feather pillow. This home had obviously been built for ministers with big families. It fairly cried out for children to fill its hallways and many rooms.

She felt a pang of guilt again. She wouldn't be the woman to give the current minister those children. She was only breezing into his life for a short time.

Feeling restless, needing to clear her head, she changed into warm clothes, grabbed her cameras and went out back to explore.

Her boots crunched over the patchy snow. Breathing in the crisp winter air, ever watchful for life around her, she snapped photos of everything, from blades of grass to the scuttling clouds in the sky, never censoring her choices or thinking twice, having learned that amazement could result from what appeared totally mundane. Every shot, no matter how seemingly insignificant, had the potential to be the next big break.

And Amy believed with all her heart that someday, the coveted Pulitzer Prize would be hers. She wanted it with a fierceness she could taste.

"For you, Dad," she whispered.

She didn't question a single impulse that compelled her to depress the shutter.

When she came to the frozen creek, she paused, the thin ice reminding her of her father's sacrifice, and now Dan's.

"No sense dwelling," she said aloud. "What's done is done."

The clear two-note whistle of a chickadee drew her attention. Perched atop the gray branch of a naked cottonwood tree, she might have missed the bird if not for its inky-black feathery cap and bib. The tiny chickadee ruffled its white-edged wings and burst into carefree song. *Fee-beee, fee-beee.*

Adjusting the focus and light on the Nikon, she went down on one knee, uncaring as damp earth seeped through the fabric of her jeans. Against the vast blue sky, the little bird clung to the spindly branches of the tree like a rope climber shimmying for purchase.

A hand on her shoulder startled her and she blew the next shot.

Dan put a finger to his lips and pointed to the left. A doe wandered down from a knoll, paused. Used to watching, waiting, Amy remained still, her camera poised. She got off a few shots, deciding she would underexpose the film, give the image a muted cast rather than sharp clarity.

She didn't expect the animal to come close enough for the perfect shot. She could smell the subtle sandalwood scent of Dan's cologne, the same scent that had engulfed her senses when he'd kissed her at the wedding, the same scent that still filled her mind.

The deer would catch the scent, too.

Sure enough, the creature lifted her head, nose to the wind, then darted back the way she'd come. Amy lowered her camera.

"That would have been a beautiful shot if she'd come closer," he said.

"She knew we were here."

"I didn't see her looking."

"She smelled us. One of us is wearing cologne."

"Sorry." He gave her a sheepish look. "I didn't think I'd used a heavy hand."

Lest he think she was criticizing, she smiled. "You didn't. And it's very nice."

"Nice to catch a woman, but not a deer."

Her heart bumped in her chest. His penchant for blurting out things like that continually caught her off guard.

"Were you hoping to catch a woman?" Had he especially worn that sexy scent for her?

"Looks like I already did."

He'd changed out of his suit and was back to looking like a hunky cowboy. Used to working around men, Amy didn't normally respond to a pretty face or flirty come-on. With Dan, that's all she seemed able to do. Respond.

Cryin' all night.

Deciding it wasn't wise to pursue this line of conversation, she changed the subject. "You didn't stay in the study for long. Did you finish the sermon?"

"I had a little trouble concentrating."

"I'm sorry. I guess we both feel a little uncomfortable."

"Speak for yourself. Now me, I just figured it was remiss of me to leave you on your own so soon."

His tone was easy and light. And darn it all, flirty. What was the matter with him? It seemed utterly ridiculous to suggest that they set some rules of conduct—for all she knew, he flirted with every woman and she was merely overreacting. For goodness' sake, the man was an absolute enigma.

"You don't have to change your life for me."

"I don't intend to. Nothing says I can't take a break and do a little moonlighting as a tour guide."

The only thing remotely resembling a tourist attraction was a ranch house off in the distance, looking small and insignificant against the vast landscape. "Not much touring. It's so flat, you can see for miles. But it's beautiful."

"Yes. Let's walk a bit." With a hand beneath her elbow, he gallantly helped her to her feet and steered her along the bank of the frozen creek, where patchy snow clung to the ground, shoots of brown grass poking through. The smell of damp earth and wood smoke from nearby chimneys permeated the air.

"Whose ranch is that over yonder?"

"Chance and Kelly Hammond's. When we were buddies growing up, Chance's family had a big outfit about five miles outside of town. Then Judith decided to open the gallery in Helena, so they sold the place because Chance didn't want the responsibility of a big ranch. He bought that place because it was closer to town."

"He and Kelly are newly married."

"Yes. And they have a couple of the cutest girls. We've claimed the littlest one as our Christmas miracle. She didn't speak when she came to town, her little voice trapped in silence over the horror of seeing her father get electrocuted."

"Oh, my gosh, how awful."

"Mmm. But the power of love and faith is amazing. The children in town kept insisting they were seeing an angel."

"Do you believe angels exist?"

He smiled. "Don't forget who you're talking to here."

Yes, she had forgotten. "Are you saying you saw one?"

"Christmas Eve. We were all gathered in town around the Christmas tree. And for the first time in six months, little Kimberly Anderson pointed and spoke. We were all so moved and astonished by her voice, we weren't sure what we'd seen."

Amy felt chills race over her arms. "What did she look like? The angel?"

"A lot like Ozzie Peyton's late wife, Vanessa."

"You're pulling my leg."

He raised his hand as though giving an oath. "Miracles are around every corner, Amy. We just get too caught up in life to look for them."

They walked in silence for a while, Amy thinking about phenomena and things that couldn't be explained away tidily and rationally.

Like why a person found themselves at a shaky crossroads in the map of life. If, as Dan believed, there was a divine purpose in everything.

"See that knoll over there?" he said, pointing. "That's the original Shotgun Ridge. You can't see it from here, but on the other side is the founding Malone's old homestead."

"It's still intact?"

"Of course. It's our historical monument. The cowboys around here use it as a line shack every once in a while, but it's our main claim to history. When weather takes its toll, different folks will step in and do repairs."

"This would be Wyatt Malone's ancestors?"

"Mmm, watch your step." He steered her around a patch of scrubby sage.

"So why isn't this Malone City or something instead of Shotgun Ridge?"

"Ah, I'm glad you asked."

She felt a smile bloom inside her. This man loved to tell a story.

"Back in the 1800s, William Malone fell in love with the land and decided this was where he'd build his family a home. He had a vision, and since there was talk of a railroad coming through not far from here, he left his wife and three kids at the homestead and went off to sell a string of mustangs to get money to build a town and hopefully convince other folks to join him."

"That seems like a big undertaking. To build a town."

"Hard for us to imagine, perhaps. Anyway, Addie Malone was as brave as she was beautiful. William had been gone several weeks when a renegade band of thieves showed up. Determined to protect her kids and her land, she did what was needed. And when William rode up, along with several other families he'd persuaded to join him, the sight that greeted them was Addie Malone, standing strong and proud on the ridge behind the house, a shotgun still in her hands and five dead thieves on the ground. They had their first town meeting right then and there and agreed that their new town would be called Shotgun Ridge.''

Amy smiled. She could picture it in her mind, depicted in a photograph, a brave woman in a simple shirtwaist dress to her ankles, the light of battle and a mother's love in her eyes.

"The Malone children have quite a role model to live up to.''

"They're up to the task. We all are since this is our town. Though I have to say we've taken a fair amount of lecturing from Ozzie Peyton over it lately. I'm surprised he didn't grab you right away and tell you the story of Addie Malone.''

"Why?''

"It's a campaign he and his buddies have undertaken. A couple of years ago, he and his pals formed what we're now fondly calling the matchmaker group, claiming it was a sad thing that a woman was responsible for guarding and naming the town, yet the community had dwindled down to predominantly a male population. They set out to draw women here, took out ads for mail-order brides and organized a bachelor auction. They've meddled and maneuvered without shame.''

"It appears to have worked. I saw plenty of women and children at Brewer's the other night…and today.''

He grinned. "Yes. I must admit, I found myself unwittingly drawn into the plans a time or two. I like it, though, what's happening to our town. It does my heart good to see it blossoming again. I can't imagine living anyplace else.''

The pride in his voice when he spoke of his town was unmistakable. ''Did you always feel this way? Know you wanted to set down roots?''

''Probably. Though as a teen I didn't give it much thought, took it for granted. What about you? Didn't you feel your roots tied to Georgia?''

''No. I focused on Dad's travels, couldn't wait to pack my bags and follow in his footsteps. From the time I was a little girl, that's been my dream. I made maps and hung them on my bedroom wall, stuck pins in the places he'd been, charted each course he took. His life was a grand adventure. He'd call at night, describe it all to me, what he'd seen through the lens of his camera, the people he'd met.''

''Seductive.''

She jolted, didn't expect him to use descriptive words like that. But the description was right on target.

It also accurately depicted the gaze he directed down at her, the complete focus he gave her.

''Yes,'' she whispered. ''Very seductive.''

For the longest moment, they stared at each other. Then Amy stepped back.

She was reading things into a turn of phrase or a look that simply weren't there.

For pity's sake, the blinding knowledge that this was her wedding day was playing with her mind. That's all there was to it.

And it was going to stop. Right now.

In name only, Amy. Remember it.

Now, if this sexy preacher would just quit looking at her as though she were a blonde in a Corvette convertible, she might survive these next three months.

Chapter Six

At the rate she was going, Amy figured she'd have a bleeding ulcer when her three months were up and would end up blowing her shot at the *National Geographic* job.

It was Sunday morning. She was the preacher's wife, about to hear her husband give a sermon. She didn't imagine it would go over well with folks if she skipped church the day after she'd married their minister.

What was she supposed to wear?

Oh, Gramps, what were you thinking?

Her wardrobe ranged from one end of the scale to the other—risqué to sloppy-casual, with very little in between. The risqué items were due to her night job, the casual ones geared toward her photography career needs.

Respectable preacher's wife dresses were as noticeably scarce in her closet as bird droppings in a cuckoo clock.

Well, never let it be said she was a woman who wouldn't ask directions. Tightening the satin sash on her robe, she barreled out of her room and ran smack-dab into a solid wall of masculine flesh.

"Oh, my gosh. I didn't expect to…"

"Likewise. Is the house on fire?"

If it had been, she couldn't have moved to save her own life.

The man only wore a towel around his waist.

His chest was wide and firm beneath her hands, covered by a light sprinkling of mahogany hair, and his skin was warm and damp. He smelled of soap and shampoo.

Through the thin layer of her silk robe and the terry-cloth towel, it was impossible not to feel his reaction to their unexpected encounter.

A typical male reaction of arousal.

The body contact sent a pulse of desire racing from her belly straight to her femininity. She flushed and jumped away from him like a scalded cat, determined not to cast her gaze downward to verify the ridge of desire her body had felt.

She cleared her throat, looked away. "Um, I was coming to find out what to wear."

"Anything you like."

How could he just stand there and speak so calmly? Especially since he was, well… "Help me out here. What are you wearing?"

"A towel at the moment."

That's all it took. Her eyes dipped down. She groaned.

"Amy—"

She held up her hand. "I know. You're a man. It's

just...I hadn't counted on...oh, damn it, never mind. What are you *going* to wear to *church?*"

He smiled. "Testy in the mornings, I see."

"Would you just hush up and answer the question so I can go hide in the nearest hole for the next century or so?"

That sent him into a gale of laugher. "Please don't. I'd have to answer way too many questions about your disappearance."

She curled her fingers into her sweaty palms. Looking at his bare chest wasn't helping her any more than looking at the front of his towel. Her fantasies were having a field day.

"Clothes, Dan," she reminded.

"Hmm. I never knew roommates discussed wardrobes. This is new to me."

"Yes, well, pretend I'm your sister and help me out."

His gazed rested on her hair, caught up in a messy ponytail. "I only had brothers."

She glared at him. "Pretend."

He laughed. "Let's see. I had in mind my gray suit with the white shirt. I've got a cool tie that the ladies give me plenty of compliments on—has red chili peppers and little bottles of hot sauce on it...what?" he asked, obviously responding to her frown. "You don't think that's appropriate?"

"No. I'm sure it's fine." Her mind was racing over a mental inventory of her clothes. Why hadn't she planned for this?

Cryin' all night, she'd come here to be a preacher's wife.

That meant going to church, being respectable.

"I just thought maybe…that people might be a little more, uh, casual."

"Ah. This is a dress or pants question, right?"

"'Fraid so. And you get extra points if you say pants."

He laughed and didn't appear to have any trouble letting his gaze settle on the contours of her body beneath the robe.

Honestly, she was trying so hard not to ogle *him*. The least he could do was return the favor.

"Folks wear pretty much what they want. We're not formal. When it's cold like this, we opt for comfort. So, anything you wear will be fine. This is a come-as-you-are church, with the emphasis on *coming*."

Her jaw went slack.

She was certain he hadn't meant that in a sexual way. But given the undercurrents arcing between them in the hallway, and the way his arousal had moments ago tented the front of his towel, that's exactly how she took it.

With a hand gripping the lapels of her robe, she mumbled a thank-you and fled back to the safety of her room, wishing like mad she wasn't going to have to face him again.

In the church.

"Oh, Lord, this is a mess. Give me strength."

DAN LEFT THE HOUSE early so he'd be on hand to greet the congregation. He'd hated to leave Amy on her own, but he didn't have any idea how long she'd take to get ready. He didn't picture her as the type to primp, but she'd been especially flustered this morning and had nearly taken his head off when he'd knocked on her bedroom door after their hallway encounter.

Man alive, that particular escapade was going to give him a bad moment or two. He was sure of it. His concentration was zip to none.

By rote, he shook Stony Stratton's hand when the other man stopped on the threshold of the sanctuary, then forgot to release it.

As though he'd been struck dumb, blind and mute, he froze.

Amy stood uncertainly at the bottom of the church steps.

She wore a pair of brown slacks and a beige scooped-neck top. The material of both items apparently included a healthy percentage of spandex, because they hugged her curves in a way that was even sexier than the silky robe he'd last seen her in had been.

Chic and sexy, he thought. Beautiful. A soft cardigan sweater hung open over her top, skimming her breasts. Her lips shimmered with coral gloss and she'd swept her rich chestnut hair into an updo that screamed sensuality when he was certain she'd been aiming for sedate.

"You might want to turn loose of my hand," Stony commented dryly. "Folk'll start to talk."

"What? Oh, sorry." He laughed to cover the turmoil in his gut. *Get a grip, man.*

"No need to be. I have the same problem when my own wife walks into a room."

"She's not..." Dan decided to shut his mouth. He'd been about to say she wasn't his wife. But she was. For now.

Stony went inside and Dan looked down at Amy. She still stood frozen at the bottom of the church steps. Well, good. No sense in him being the only one impersonating a statue.

His male ego wanted to believe it was the sight of him that caused her hesitation. His rational mind told him it was the unfamiliar situation.

He raised his brows and held out a hand. "You coming in?"

"If you insist."

He grinned. He really did enjoy this woman. "I promise we don't sacrifice beautiful women at the altar. You'll be safe." He took her hand and helped her up the last step. "You look very nice."

A twinkle of mischief sparkled in her green eyes. "Evidently better than nice. You, Pastor Dan, were staring."

"Guilty. Now say 'Thank you, Dan, for the compliment.'"

"Thank you, Dan, for the compliment."

"Just what I like. An obedient woman."

"In your dreams, pal."

His laughter rang out as he led her inside, causing heads to turn and smiles to light up. "Spunky, too."

"Oh, hush up, will you?"

"Yes, ma'am. Come with me."

"Where?"

"To sit down so we can get this show on the road."

Her hand whipped out and wrapped around the post of an empty pew, nearly pulling his arm out of the socket as she brought them up short. He had to do some fancy footwork to backtrack.

"I can just scoot right in here."

"I have a rule in my church. No one's allowed to sit in the back row unless there's standing room only. As you can see for yourself, the population only fills us up about three-quarters."

"Fine, I'll just—"

"Amy, when my father was pastor here, my mother always sat in the front row."

"I'm not your mother."

Major understatement. The memory of her warm body, naked beneath a satiny robe, flashed in his mind. "No, but you're my wife."

"Oh. Yes, of course. The minister's wife sits in front."

"Usually. Unless she's playing the piano, but that job's already filled by Kelly Hammond."

"Good thing. I can't play a note."

"Then we won't ask you to. And if it'll make you uncomfortable, you don't have to sit up front."

She sighed, and his gaze was drawn to the way her chest rose and fell.

Oh, man.

Maybe it would be better all around if she *did* sit in the back—behind the tallest man in the congregation.

"No. I'm fine."

That made one of them. He wasn't so sure about himself.

Amy compromised and sat in the second row next to Emily and Cheyenne Bodine. She gazed at the twin babies, one dressed in blue, the other in pink, and smiled. They were cuties, both sleeping like angels.

"Morning, Miz Lucas," Cheyenne said.

Amy frowned and looked around. Then she realized he meant her. Lucas. Amy Lucas. That was her.

"Um…good morning." This was crazy. The whole town knew the reason for the marriage. To fulfill the obligation of a will.

They also knew she'd married the *preacher*. She'd thought it was understood that this was simply an expediency sort of thing.

Then why did it feel as though every word spoken or look given or question asked came with a gently knowing tone?

It was like a conspiracy, and her…her *husband* was in fine form, as well, teasing, using sexual innuendo like…like *coming*. *This is a come-as-you-are church, with the emphasis on coming.*

With her hands clasped primly in her lap, knees together and heels flat on the floor, she sat like a statue guarding a nickel arcade, and watched Dan's killer smile and infectious laughter light up the room.

He thanked the Malones for the donation of the flowers, advised everyone not to get carried away as he invited the congregation to stand up and greet their neighbor, then openly teased Kelly Hammond by telling her he was going to introduce a new hymn they didn't have sheet music for, just to see if she could keep up.

Everyone laughed and Kelly challenged him to do his best.

Emily Bodine leaned across her husband to get Amy's attention. "Kelly was one of those gifted children," she explained. "She skipped high school and went right into college then medical school. She also plays the piano beautifully and can pick up most any tune by ear. Dan's been trying to outfox her every Sunday morning."

Amy grinned and whispered back, "Has he succeeded?"

"Not yet."

Like the marriage ceremony yesterday, the church service today was a bit unorthodox, with people talking out of turn, making comments and engaging Dan in teasing debates that had nothing to do with Bible teaching and everything to do with playfulness, love and community spirit.

Soon enough, though, he regained order and segued into a sermon.

As he had when he'd related the story of his and Amy's fathers, he made the message come alive. He spoke about making one's life count, infusing the Parable of The Talents from the book of Matthew with vivid images, putting his own spin on what the characters of old might have been thinking and feeling. He tapped into imagery every person present could relate to.

He didn't preach fire and brimstone, didn't judge or come on strong, didn't promise they were all going to hell in a handbasket if they didn't straighten up and fly right.

Instead, he spoke of riches and everyone's right to them, monetary riches and life's riches. The riches of love.

He held the congregation spellbound, a showman who laughed often, lost his place a time or two when he got off track telling a joke, and Amy gained a new respect for Dan Lucas.

Laughter. He embodied the emotion, inspired it in others. It was a seductive trait, as much a part of him as his name.

She felt as though she could watch him for hours.

A little bit of the bad boy he'd once been crept out now and again in a crazy joke or an example conveyed using a story from his own life. He never lost sight of the fact that he was human, no different than anyone else, and that made him a great teacher.

It also made it doubly hard for Amy to rein in her thoughts. His suit fit him like a dream. His whimsical tie with chili peppers and Tabasco bottles negated the formality of the starched white shirt and gray wool jacket. His shoulders were so broad he needed no padding.

She knew that firsthand. And the memory of his warm, naked skin sent a flush of heat to her cheeks.

A sexy, flirtatious bad boy preaching a sermon.

Every one of her preconceived notions flew out the window.

He evoked fantasies she shouldn't be having.

Suddenly, in midsentence, he faltered, and Amy realized his gaze had collided with hers.

She sucked in a breath, tried to pretend she hadn't been caught staring at him like a teenager with a mad crush on a music idol.

He recovered quicker than she did. Even from this distance, she could see the twinkle in his eye.

He *knew* what she was thinking.

By darn, this man set her nerves on fire with a mere look. It was as though he knew a secret that only the two of them shared—a sexual secret.

It was unnerving.

He flustered her, made her anticipate. And she felt majorly guilty for the direction of her thoughts.

Especially in church.

Especially since that's not what this relationship was about.

"THAT'S THE EATIN'EST CHURCH I've ever been to," Amy said when they got home. "After yesterday, I never imagined there'd be a potluck again today. Do the ladies here ever get out of the kitchen?"

"Amazing, isn't it. A single man in town won't go hungry. He just has to come to church, and he's set for the week."

His body certainly didn't show a tendency to overeat. Flat stomach, shirt tucked in, nice pecs. "Is that how it's been for you? Do the females in your flock keep you fed and stocked with casseroles?"

"The females in my flock?" He laughed. "Remember the story I told you about the meddlers' campaign? Until a couple of years ago, the bachelors outnumbered the women in this town. I'll have you know I'm fairly adept at finding my way around a kitchen."

"A man of many talents."

"I like to think so."

A certain inflection in the deepening of his voice made her heart flutter. She wished she could get a handle on this man. He confused her, intrigued her...excited her.

She reached up and started removing pins from her hair. "Speaking of kitchens—or there about—I was wondering if you'd mind if I appropriated the laundry room to set up a darkroom. It's got the sink, plenty of counter space and no windows, so I can close it off."

"Sure. I told you to make yourself at home, and I meant it. Just let me know the rules so I don't mess up your film if I stumble in to wash my dirty socks."

"If the door's closed, knock first. I'll let you know if it's safe to enter."

"So, you take your own pictures and develop them, too?"

She noticed that he was watching her remove the hairpins, realized that her raised arms caused her top to stretch even tighter across her breasts. She shouldn't have started, but it was too late to stop now.

"Yes. The equipment was expensive, but I've accumulated it little by little. And it works out cheaper in the long run, gives me the advantage of choosing which negatives are worth developing and which ones can be scrapped." She set the bobby pins on the table, ran her fingers through her unbound hair and winced when her scalp stung from hair follicles being forced at an unnatural angle.

"Hurt?"

"Mmm."

"Here, you missed one." He plucked a stray pin from her hair and allowed his fingers to linger for a moment, to massage.

Amy went utterly still. His fingers felt wonderful against her scalp, raised chills on her arms.

She stepped back, ducked her head. *Think about darkrooms, Amy, ones that you develop film in.* "Um…thanks."

"Anytime. Can I do anything to help you set up?"

She started to refuse automatically, then decided that was silly. "Sure, you can use your muscles to haul in those boxes I stacked by the front door. But let's go change clothes first."

She had him by the arm and was urging him toward the stairs before she realized what she was doing. She dropped her hand.

"I mean…you go change—if you want. I'll go…I'll just go to my own room and—"

"Amy?"

"Yes. I know. I'm babbling."

"And why is that?"

"Because you make me nervous."

He grinned.

"Are you doing it deliberately?"

"Maybe. I like the way that Southern accent goes all soft and fluttery, the way you bite your lip when you're flustered."

"And here I thought you were a gentleman."

He winked at her. "That's what you get for thinking."

Whistling, he jogged up the stairs. What had he

meant by that? It was almost as though he was giving her a fair warning.

But a warning for what? That he wasn't going to play by the rules?

Cryin' all night. One of them needed to have a little strength of resistance. And she'd been counting on *him* being the one to have it since *she* felt like a hormone-laden weakling.

AMY HAD HER EQUIPMENT laid out, and trays lined up and ready for the developer, stop bath and fixer solutions. Removing the white incandescent lamp in the overhead fixture, she screwed a red bulb into the socket and gave a burst of laughter when it cast a glow over the room that resembled a bawdy bordello.

"Great, I've just created a red-light district in the rectory."

A knock at the open doorway made her jump.

Dan, grinning like a sexy bad boy, leaned against the jamb. "I agree. That might raise a few eyebrows."

"I didn't see you there."

"I know. You were busy imagining cathouses."

"Well, since I'm fairly certain you're not standing in line to be a customer, what's up?"

"I wanted to let you know I'm going out to the reservation. I've got a collection of food and second-hand clothes to deliver."

Amy automatically grabbed her camera and looped it over her neck, checked the supplies in her backpack. "Can I come...I mean *go* with you?" Darn it.

She was going to have to get past the double meaning of that word.

"I thought you were going to develop pictures."

"Not when I have a chance to get outside and explore."

He gestured gallantly with his arm that she should precede him. "Then by all means, let's go explore." He glanced at the red lightbulb, shook his head and grinned, then flipped off the switch.

"Bordellos in the rectory," he muttered. "What next?"

"Oh, stop teasing me. The red light allows me to see what I'm doing and keeps the film from being ruined."

He laughed. "I'm pretty sure I knew that."

Digging her keys out of her backpack, she went straight to her Jeep.

"Uh, Amy?" He raised a brow and held open the passenger door of his four-wheel-drive crew cab truck.

"Oh. You're driving."

"Aside from the fact that it makes me feel manly, the supplies are already loaded in here."

She slipped beneath his arm and climbed into the truck. "Manly, huh?"

His gaze connected with hers. "Yeah."

He'd flustered her. He could tell by the way her breath stilled, by the way her eyes widened and her mouth went slack.

He wasn't sure why he felt compelled to flirt with her, to bait her. She brought out a side of him he hadn't indulged in for longer than he could remember.

A PRETTY, DARK-EYED WOMAN beamed when Amy and Dan walked into the recreation center to deliver the donated supplies.

"Dan! I was about to give up on you." The young woman gave him a warm hug, laughing when the box he held in his arms got in the way.

Amy set the crate she was holding onto the floor.

"Lily Gray Squirrel, this is Amy," Dan introduced. "Amy, Lily."

She shook hands with the other woman. Lily was polite enough, but dismissed Amy right away and turned back to Dan.

Amy wasn't insulted. Dan had a way of lighting up a room and commanding attention. Curious, though, that he'd mentioned Lily's last name, but not hers. Then again, why would he introduce her as his wife when it wasn't the real thing and would cause unneeded explanations?

She watched the interaction between Lily and Dan. He was friendly and joking. A toucher. Not sexually. He was simply social. He cared.

And Lily Gray Squirrel was smitten.

That was obvious from the gentle looks she sent Dan's way, and the daggers she shot at Amy when he wasn't looking.

Had her sudden presence in his life messed up something between him and this beautiful woman?

Deciding to take herself out of the line of fire, Amy slipped out the door and went to explore.

Losing herself in the atmosphere, she took pictures of the homes and the people.

A mud-encrusted dog lay stretched out on his side

on a front porch, his muscles twitching as he no doubt dreamed of a rabbit he'd chased that had worn him out and necessitated a rejuvenating nap.

An old man sitting in a rocking chair gazed off in the distance as though remembering a time when he was a strong young brave or pining for a loved one. A soiled bandanna rode his forehead, taming a head of long gray hair that resembled thin strands of gauzy cotton.

She adjusted her focus, zooming in on gray whiskers poking out of a face etched by history and eyes that reflected hardship, wisdom, pride and an aching emptiness that brought tears to her own eyes.

The urge to sit with him, ask him to share his stories, was strong, but she didn't want to intrude. So, she simply smiled and waved when he caught her watching him, then pivoted at the sound of children's voices.

A group of little girls with dark braids shrieked happily as they tossed a beanbag marker into a hopscotch square and teetered on one leg, trying to pick it up without putting their other foot on the ground.

Amy remembered entertaining herself for hours out in back of her grandparents' house, with nothing more than ten chalk-drawn squares and a rock as a marker.

"Hey, lady. You wanna play?"

Amy lowered her camera and grinned. "Absolutely."

DAN LEANED AGAINST the post of a nearby porch and watched Amy. When he'd left the rec center on his way to visit the Lightfoot family, he'd seen her playing hopscotch with the children in the street, laughing and screeching when she'd lost her balance and landed on the chalk line rather than the square.

He imagined the extra burden of anchoring her camera against her chest with one hand had thrown off her equilibrium—or else she'd done it deliberately so as not to show up the children.

Jenny White Cloud, smiling over the antics of the strange woman in town, had beckoned to Amy. Satisfied that she was okay on her own, Dan had gone about his business—rushed it actually—his mind on Amy.

She was still where he'd seen her last, in the midst of a circle of women who were teaching her the art of weaving.

He watched the way she bit her bottom lip, concentrated, laughed at herself when she tangled the yarn and had to fish the wooden shuttle back through and try again. She was a good sport, a participant.

He recalled how she'd jumped in to help out at Brewer's on her first day here when the crowd had grown and there hadn't been enough hands to do the work.

And every opportunity that presented itself, she recorded on her camera.

He wondered if she realized that by engaging these people in conversation—people who were strangers to her—showing an interest, she was behaving exactly as a minister's wife would.

He decided to keep that observation to himself. Because he wasn't sure how he felt about it.

Allowing himself to get attached, to feel pride,

wouldn't serve any purpose when she left this all behind three months from now.

Still, in record time, his new wife was getting under his skin.

Chapter Seven

"So, how have you managed to remain single all these years?" In the truck on the way home, Amy couldn't get the image of Dan and Lily's warm good-bye out of her mind.

"Are you asking if I've dated?"

Or had sex. *Oh, Amy, please!* "I guess. Lily Gray Squirrel comes to mind."

He glanced at her. "Lily? We're just friends."

"Not according to her."

"She said something?"

"She didn't have to. Cryin' all night, Dan, the woman's half in love with you. Surely you've seen it."

He sighed. "She's young."

"All the more reason you shouldn't encourage her unless you mean business."

Now he frowned. "I don't encourage her."

"Not deliberately. You're a natural toucher. You give a woman your complete attention, make her feel as though she's the only woman in your universe at the time."

"Are we still talking about Lily?"

She glared at him. "I'm making an observation. And I think I'm fairly qualified, since I spend so much of my time studying people and their nuances."

"For a minute there, I thought you might be jealous."

"Get real."

He laughed. "I'm glad you pointed out Lily's feelings to me. I'd suspected, but wasn't sure. I've never treated her any differently than I do anyone else, but a couple of times I've had a little jolt of unease."

"One should generally pay attention to jolts of unease."

"Yes, ma'am. As to your question about dating, it's been a while. Aside from the lack of time and single ladies here in town, I've found that woman are often scared off by my vocation. They figure either a minister doesn't know how or is against having a good time."

"You're kidding. How can anyone know you for more than five minutes and not realize you like to have fun?"

"Beats me. It's that title thing, I suppose. Even you reacted to it, if you recall."

"Guilty."

"I walk into a room and people still hide their lit cigarettes."

"From a cigar-smoking preacher?"

"Not everyone knows I indulge," he said in a stage whisper as though a crowd of gossipy eavesdroppers were hiding in the back seat, ears cocked. "Oh, looks like we've got company."

They drove up in front of the house just as a white

truck with the green Callahan and Sons logo on the door panel was pulling away from the barn, a horse trailer hitched to the back.

Dan braked and rolled down the window as Grant Callahan pulled abreast of them.

"Ethan said you were looking to borrow a gentle mount," Grant said. "I put Clarabelle in your barn. She should do right by you."

"Thanks, Grant. Tell Ethan I appreciate the loan."

Dan rolled up the window and waved as Grant's rig slowly navigated the narrow road beside the church.

"You're borrowing a horse?"

"You ride, don't you?"

"It's been a while, but yes."

"Good. I figured it'd be nicer if you had your own mount. Easier than have you ride double with me on Moses's rump."

"Were we planning to ride together?"

"I had it on the agenda, yes." He shut off the engine and got out of the truck.

Amy released her seat belt and followed. "Are you determined to entertain me?"

He seemed to think about that for a minute. "I guess I am."

She looked at the house, the church beyond that, then back at the barn. "I do feel a little like a guest. This hasn't really sunk in yet. But you can't play host for the next three months."

"No. But every newly married couple deserves a honeymoon. Maybe that's what I'm giving you."

Her heart vaulted into her throat. "You're not...I mean, you don't expect it to lead to—"

He laughed and tugged at her hair. "Woman, you think about, talk about and allude to sex more than anyone I've come across in a long time."

Affronted, embarrassed because he was very likely right, she countered, "I do not."

He stepped closer, his voice dropped. "No? Maybe it's that lack of a love life you were lamenting the day you got here."

She sucked in a breath. "That just came out of nowhere. I didn't mean it."

"Mmm. But it's stuck in my mind. Can't help it. Can't get rid of it. So, let's see where it goes."

See where it...?

He tipped up her chin and her palms went damp, her mouth dry.

His deep brown eyes were filled with an intent that was all too easy to read.

He held her with his gaze alone, waited until he had her full attention, until he was sure they were on the same page.

His thumb stroked her jaw, made a pass over her bottom lip, his gaze following, focusing on her mouth, then slowly, ever so slowly, lifted back to her eyes.

He didn't sneak up on her, didn't chase her face or act out of aggression.

He got her attention. Slowly. Thoroughly.

Then watching her, gauging her reactions, her readiness, he lowered his head and kissed her.

His actions were those of a confident man. A man

sure of his masculinity, of his skill, of his effect on a woman.

A man who knew when he was welcome.

And, oh, he was. Welcome. Skilled. He'd had some practice at this, made her feel like an absolute novice, made her yearn to see what he could teach her.

Stunned, Amy stared at him for a full five seconds when he lifted his head, took another three seconds to clear her mind.

"Oh, my goodness. Is that allowed?"

His smile was slow and sexy. "You're going to have to get over these preconceived ideas you have of me."

I'm a man.

He didn't bother to repeat the words as he'd done so many times before. Didn't need to. They were implied.

And proved. Oh, how they were proved.

"So, what do you think?"

"Um, very nice."

"I mean about the horseback ride. But thank you for the compliment. It's good for my ego."

"I have a strong suspicion your ego's just fine as it is."

He grinned. "Well? Want to saddle up and take a ride."

More than you know. Oh, for pity's sake.

She tugged at her denim jacket, took a breath and headed for the barn. There was surely a sin in having impure fantasies about a minister.

Regardless that the minister in question was her husband.

They were *not* going to consummate this union. No matter how much her hormones screamed otherwise.

When she left in three months' time, Dan Lucas would be entitled to his annulment. That was fair. That was her bargain.

And she intended to stick to it.

Now, if she could get a little cooperation from the man in question, life would run relatively smoothly.

Yeah, right. And a blind chicken would find a kernel of corn in a hayloft.

AFTER TWO WEEKS, Amy was starting to feel a little more at home, a little more relaxed. Since that second kiss by the barn, she'd gone out of her way to keep things impersonal between them, to treat him like a roommate.

It hadn't been easy.

Her saving grace came in the form of Dan's schedule. In his business, he was on call twenty-four hours a day. At least three times last week, she'd heard the phone ring in the middle of the night, heard his footsteps on the stairs as pastoral duties sent him out in the cold to counsel or comfort whomever had a need.

She didn't ask him where he went. She was afraid the sharing would create an intimacy she was trying desperately to avoid.

But she watched. And she worried. People in need were wearing him out, dumping their woes onto his shoulders. Granted, they were wide, compassionate shoulders, but she couldn't help wondering who he could turn to when he needed to unburden.

Sighing, she got back to work. She'd been ignoring

the roll of film with the wedding pictures on it for two weeks now. She wasn't sure why, but every time she reached for it, her hands hesitated, began to tremble.

Ridiculous. She might as well see if any of them were in focus. Dora Callahan had been in charge of the camera, and she'd seen for herself that Dora had a good grasp of photography. The woman's main area of expertise, thought was art. Dora drew the cutest pictures of animals, which she sold to greeting card companies.

Telling herself to stop being a ninny and get on with it, Amy developed the negatives and transferred the thumbnail images to a contact sheet, then picked up a loupe to view what was there.

She loved to work with black-and-white film. The images were so much sharper, more dramatic. For the *National Geographic* job, she would use some color film as well, but here in Montana, she didn't have the expensive equipment required for developing color film.

Just as well. The images she saw through her loupe were spectacular.

Her heart lurched when she got to the eighth frame, her stomach fluttering like a migration of monarch butterflies. She didn't bother to look at the rest.

Rushing now, cautioning herself to slow down, she located the correct negative and put it in the enlarger, adjusting the knobs until she was satisfied with the magnification, then switched off the focus light, leaving on only the red overhead bulb as she cut a test strip, then finished processing the print, gently agitating it through the developer, stop bath and fixer. Flipping on the overhead light, she gave the five-by-seven glossy a final rinse and wiped it dry with a squeegee.

Heart in her mouth, her breath coming faster than was warranted, she stared at the black-and-white image before her.

It was a photo taken seconds before their wedding kiss.

Dan had her face cupped in his hands, looking down at her. The emotions captured in that single moment in time were incredibly moving, incredibly confusing.

It was a perfect shot, in perfect focus, more powerful than if Dora had waited five seconds more and snapped the actual kiss.

Amy had seen her grandmother and grandfather in this same exact pose, wearing this same exact look as Gramps had cornered Grandma in the kitchen.

Honey, babe, you're the light of my life, Gramps had murmured an instant before he'd gently kissed her.

Even as a young girl peeking around the corner, she'd known that look was special.

How could she be seeing that same expression on her and Dan's faces at a time when they'd only known each other for two days?

Hands trembling, she took off her gloves, slipped the photograph out of sight in a binder, cleaned up her mess, then shut off the light and left the room.

She needed some air to clear her head and to reflect on why her husband in name only had looked at her as if she was the love of his life.

And why she'd mirrored that look.

If she didn't watch her step, she'd likely find herself in a wild bull's pasture without a tree.

Thinking Dan had gone out to attend to pastoral duties, she was dismayed to find him in the barn. Since he was the center of her turmoil, she'd hoped to be alone with the horses.

"Hey," he said. "Come to give me a hand mucking stalls?"

"Might as well. I could use the exercise."

"Been holed up in that darkroom. Got a few kinks, huh?"

"A few."

"Get any good pictures?"

"A few."

He paused, crossed his gloved hands atop the pitchfork and looked at her. "Well, you're a font of talkativeness today."

She smiled. "Is that even a word?"

"Beats me. What gives?"

"Nothing. It just takes me a little time to warm up after I've been cooped up working." Or been stunned by an unexpected photograph.

"You're sure?"

She walked over and took the pitchfork from his hands, nearly knocking him off balance. Despite her seesaw emotions, his concern touched her.

"You're good at listening to people's problems."

"So I've been told."

"Don't you ever get tired of it? Doesn't it become a burden?"

"I don't shoulder my burdens alone," he reminded her.

"Still, doesn't it ever get to you?"

"Sometimes. Suffering's hard to take. As is sadness."

"Is that what you do when you're called out in the middle of the night? Deal with suffering and sadness?" Darn it, she'd told herself she wouldn't ask about this.

"In the middle of the night, usually. It's not all doom and gloom, though. A couple months back I went out to sit with a young girl through the birth of her child."

"You were a labor coach?"

"Yes. Lyssa Farly. Little more than a teenager, her boyfriend dropped her off at the trailer park telling her he had a home lined up for them, and never came back from his trip to the store. She spent her life in foster care, had endured unspeakable trauma and been shuffled from place to place, so she was pretty much inured to abandonment."

"Poor thing."

"As it turned out, the boyfriend had every intention of coming back for her, but a fatal accident involving black ice on the highway and a semi prevented it."

"And she was alone again. Except for you."

"It wasn't a hardship spending time with her. She'd been slapped down so many times in her life, but she kept getting right back up. She didn't rail at the world for her troubles. She just trusted that something good would be around the corner. I admired her strength and faith. Made me wonder if my own faith would have endured had I been in her shoes.''

Without realizing it, she'd put her hand on his arm, stroking as though her touch had the power to soothe. He gave so selflessly. She didn't think she had much to give back, but she wanted to try.

For three months, maybe she could be his port in the storm of life, his friend, his shoulder to lean on when the burdens on his own got too heavy.

And maybe she was fooling herself, building a need that wasn't even there. Maybe he didn't need anyone to lighten the load on those broad shoulders.

She was so used to living with a needy mother, being the one to take care, it was hard to remember that it wasn't her job to automatically come to the rescue.

''You hungry?'' he asked.

''I imagine I could eat something, though I don't know how. I've been eating so much lately, pretty soon I won't be able to fit in my clothes.''

His gaze skimmed over her denim jacket, down her red T-shirt tucked into belted jeans. ''Doesn't look like you're in any immediate danger. You fit into your clothes very nicely.''

''I wasn't fishing for a compliment.''

''No. I don't imagine you'd need to. With a face and body like that, I'd guess men have a fair amount of trouble picking up their tongues from the floor when you walk by.''

''Oh, they do not. Half the time I wear men's clothes and a ball cap. I blend in.''

''I doubt that. What about the other half?''

"The other half of what?"

"You said half the time you wear men's clothes. Probably when you're trekking around looking for pictures to take. What about when you're serving cocktails to gentlemen watching a naughty floor show? What do you wear then?"

"Lingerie." She wondered if she'd shocked him. It would serve him right. Besides, he kept her so off balance, it would be nice to turn the tables on him.

His brows lifted. "Lingerie," he repeated. "I take it that doesn't mean a flannel granny gown."

She grinned. "Send that man to the head of the class."

"So, describe it for me. Just in the interest of expanding my education, you understand."

"Use your imagination."

"Hmm. A couple of pasties and a little black G-string—"

"I serve drinks, Dan. I'm not part of the entertainment." So much for keeping him off balance.

He laughed. "Okay, a lacy black bra to go with the G—"

"A camisole and tap pants and high heels, okay? It's as modest as a shorts outfit anybody else would wear out on a hot summer day." She didn't mention that the camisole had been more of a handkerchief top tied at the back with strings that easily tugged loose.

"Now, that wasn't so hard, was it?"

She blew out a frustrated breath. "I'm not used to describing my sexy undergarments."

"So, now they're sexy undergarments, not summer clothes."

"Oh, would you just hush?"

He reached out and tugged at her hair. It was a gesture a pesky brother might do. Somehow, Dan made it seem incredibly intimate.

"I like the way your accent gets all soft and breathy when you get flustered."

"So you bait me just to hear me talk?"

He laughed again. "I didn't have sisters, but my brothers will tell anyone who'll sit still long enough to listen that I was an ornery cuss."

"Yes, well, why don't you take your ornery self in the house and fry us up a steak or something. I've a feeling I need some protein if I'm going to be able to keep up with you."

"Hey, you're the one who suggested we act like roommates. You didn't have any problem asking about my wardrobe a couple weeks ago. I figured that was an acceptable topic of conversation."

"I was inquiring about church clothes."

"And I was inquiring about work clothes."

She shook her head and gave up. She wasn't going to win this debate. Darn it all, the man was fun. Frustrating, to be sure. But fun.

Every time she tried to build expectations of how he *should* be, he shot them down like a wrecking ball against a child's building blocks. Pitifully easy.

As they walked back to the house, Amy noticed a woman standing on the back porch, cradling a baby in a plastic infant seat.

"Odd. That's Mrs. Parnelli. She lives out in the

trailer park on the outskirts of town. Next to Lyssa, the girl I was telling you about.'' His steps quickened.

Amy watched him go from a flirtatious man to a man a person would trust with their deepest secrets and hurts.

He had a gift for compassion that didn't in any way take away from his masculinity. It caused a flutter in the pit of her stomach to watch him, his different moods, the different sides to his personality.

''Mrs. Parnelli?'' Dan took the porch steps two at a time, automatically reaching out to lay a comforting hand on her shoulder. He noticed that she'd been crying.

When fresh tears filled her eyes and spilled over her lined face, he got a bad feeling. Especially when he gazed down at the baby.

Lyssa's baby. Barely three months old.

''Where's Lyssa?'' he asked gently.

''She died, Pastor.''

Grief, swift and immediate, gripped him. No. He'd just seen her last week. Young and full of plans for herself and her baby.

''Died? How?''

''Pneumonia. By the time Doc Hammond got there she was gone.''

He knew she'd been battling a stubborn cold but thought that's all it was. ''Why wasn't I called?''

''There wasn't time.''

''You were with her?'' He couldn't bear the thought that Lyssa had died alone.

''Yes. She just started coughing…couldn't catch

her breath. I didn't know what to do. It happened so fast.''

Dan glanced down at the baby, swallowed hard, felt his emotions swell.

Lyssa was gone. And this child had no one.

Lyssa had spent hours talking to him, telling him about her rough life. She had no family to support her, only the neighbors at the trailer park who watched out for her, who each took turns lending their couch for the sweet young girl to sleep on.

Moved by her plight, he'd taken up a donation and helped her buy a used eight-hundred-dollar single-wide trailer. It was a sad-looking silver bullet, but in Lyssa's eyes, it had been her cottage in the country. Each time he visited, she had a new decorating touch to show him and exclaim over.

Ellen Parnelli shifted the baby in her arms and handed him a letter written on sheet of stationery scented with perfume and outlined with a border of smiling yellow stars. Typically Lyssa. She believed in stars smiling down with promises around every corner. Amazing, after all she'd been through.

''She made me promise to give you this,'' Ellen said. ''And to bring Shayna to you.''

Dan's gaze jerked from the sweet-smelling paper in his hand to the baby, his heart rate doubling.

''Heaven knows, I would have kept the child, but I've got children of my own and there's not enough money to go around as it is,'' she apologized. ''Besides, you're the only one Lyssa ever really trusted. This is what she wanted, Pastor.''

Dan made himself focus on the words scrawled on the paper in a loopy back slant.

Dear Pastor Dan: In case something happens to me, I wanted my wishes to be known. Shayna is my sunshine and I promised I'd give her the best life a girl could have, that she'd never end up like I did, never have to worry if she was safe in her own bed, or if the rise of the sun would mean she'd have to leave one home and go to another. I want my baby to have security, to know that there's love and goodness in this world, to never have to be scared, to be raised by good people. You've been like a father to me, (I don't mean to suggest that you're old).

Dan chuckled past the emotion clogging his throat.

You're the kind of man I'd wish for the father of my baby. I want her to have everything. And I believe you're the person who can give that to her. So, please, Pastor Dan, promise me that you'll look after my Shayna if anything happens to me. Ellen Parnelli knows my wishes, and I've trusted her to bring Shayna to you. If you're reading this now, it means I'm in heaven. Until it's time for my Shayna to join me, please take care of her. Raise her for me, Pastor Dan. Keep her safe. Promise me.

With love and sincerity and gratitude,
Lyssa Farly

Dan looked at the baby in Ellen Parnelli's arms, the child fast asleep in the cradle of the infant seat, blissfully unaware of the tragedy that had touched her young life.

Had Lyssa had a premonition of what was to come when she'd written this? Had she been well and simply realizing that our grasp on life is as tenuous as a puff on a dandelion? That nothing should be taken for granted lest our plans don't coincide with what's written above?

Or had she been wheezing for breath and scared, yet holding on long enough to insure her child's future?

Lord, if she'd only called him, he would have been there for her, offered what comfort he could. But Lyssa didn't have a phone. She was proud and independent. He didn't imagine she had reached out to her neighbors until it was too late.

He glanced at Amy, who was standing a few paces away, her green eyes worried and filled with questions. She, too, was the type of woman who only reached out for help if there was no other alternative.

"Pastor Dan?" Ellen's voice was tentative, shaking with tears.

He nodded. "It's okay, Ellen."

"Thank you. Lyssa was right to trust you." She transferred the baby to him, and hooked the diaper bag on his shoulder. "Bless you, Pastor."

Sniffing, she hugged him, then gave Amy's arm a squeeze as she passed.

Feeling like a man overboard without a lifeboat, he

watched Ellen get in her compact car, then looked at Amy.

"Dan?"

He closed his eyes, swallowed hard, fought the emotions that were screaming for release.

"Looks like I've become a father as well as a husband in the space of two short weeks."

Chapter Eight

Panic washed over Amy in huge, engulfing waves as she followed Dan back inside.

"Wait a minute. This wasn't part of the deal."

"You take what you get, Amy."

In other words, he hadn't asked for marriage but had gone with it. He hadn't asked for a baby, either, but he would step up to the plate.

Their lives were accidentally entwined for the next little while. That meant she had to deal with what came into his life while she was in it, too.

And hadn't she just been thinking less than a half an hour ago that she'd try to be his rock if he needed a respite?

She mentally pushed up her sleeves. How much trouble could one little baby be in the scheme of things?

She found out several minutes later when Dan went into the study to call Cheyenne Bodine at the sheriff's office to make a report or get some advice or something.

Amy stared at the unhappy baby in the carrier, and had no idea what to do.

She was in charge. Very big mistake. Her insides were boiling at a rate that would make a pressure cooker look calm.

Dan hadn't been gone more than two minutes when the cherub in a pink bunny suit had scrunched up her little face and started squalling like a she-cat cornered by a tom in a blind alley.

As Shayna's cries got louder, Amy's last nerve frayed. What should she do?

She didn't know squat about babies, was sure she didn't have a maternal bone in her body.

She glanced frantically around the room searching for something...anything. Her gaze skimmed everything. A camelback leather sofa with nail-head trim. A matching easy chair with ottoman. Oak tables with rounded corners, no sharp edges she noted, for children to hurt themselves on. A Bible on the lamp stand beside the chair. Magazines on the coffee table. Firewood on the brick hearth. A stash of toys in the corner....

Toys?

"The man has toys," she said aloud, hoping the sound of her voice would get the baby's attention. "Why does a single man have toys in his house?"

She grabbed a stuffed elephant from the plastic crate and jumped when it squeaked.

"Just what we need. More noise." With a squeaking elephant in one hand and a little rubber duck in the other—also squeaking—she waved and cooed and squeezed.

"What the heck is all this noise?" Dan asked, striding back into the room.

"It's a cattleman's convention," she snapped, feeling as helpless as a mime in handcuffs. "What do you think it is? This child is crying to beat the band."

"Why didn't you pick her up?"

"Why don't *you* pick her up?"

"I was out of the room." He unhooked the safety restraints and gently lifted the baby in his arms.

"There, there, sweetheart. It's okay." The child shushed.

Little traitor.

The look he gave Amy was in direct contrast to the sweetly soothing tone he used on the baby.

"Well, really, Dan. I have no experience in this area."

"And you think I do?"

"More than me."

"How do you figure that?"

"At least you hold them when you christen them...or whatever it is you do."

He watched her for a long, thoughtful moment. "Where is this fear coming from?"

"Who says I'm afraid."

"You do," he said softly. "Actions speak louder than any words."

She looked away.

"Tell me."

She sighed and started to link her hands together, jumping when the forgotten elephant squeaked again. She set the toy on the table, rubbed her palms on her jeans. She was perspiring like a diva in a sauna. Helplessness and crying babies tended to do that to a girl.

"My cousin...we were little girls then, at a family

barbecue. She wasn't supposed to pick up her baby brother, but we sneaked into my mother's room, where they'd laid the baby down for a nap. I told her not to, but Trena lifted the baby off the bed. It started wriggling around, crying and flailing its arms and legs, arching backward like Gumby.''

Chills shivered through her body as she replayed the horror.

"Gramps came into the room and startled Trena, and she dropped the baby. All I could do was stand there, stunned. I was older, Gramps said he expected better of me, that I should have made Trena mind.''

"And the baby?''

"A slight concussion. Still, every time I see a little baby, my mind flashes on that image. They're so small, so helpless.''

He moved over beside her. "You were a child yourself, Amy. You're grown now. From where I'm standing, those arms look pretty buff to me. Plenty strong enough to cradle a fifteen-pound infant.''

The face was so sweet. It was an irrational fear to hang on to.

"Don't you think it's time to see what you've been missing? I guarantee you, once she cuddles into your arms you'll be hooked.''

That's what she was afraid of. She had no business getting hooked—on a husband in name only, or a child abandoned on the doorstep.

But as Dan eased the tiny little girl into her arms, she felt the hook sink into her heart, felt a sweetness, a softness unlike anything she'd ever experienced.

"She's so...warm, and soft.'' Awe washed over

her. Though her arms were stiff, she managed to stretch a finger to stroke the baby's downy cheek.

Dan draped an arm around her from behind, gazed over her shoulder at the baby. The warm heat of his body pressed against the back of her.

She went very still. The baby wiggled and fussed, and Amy's heart lurched into her throat.

"Easy. You're doing fine." He reached around her, cradling one arm beneath the baby, alongside her arm.

The baby settled.

Amy wished she could say the same thing for her galloping heart.

"What now?" she whispered.

"I called Cheyenne, apprised him of the situation and asked him to check into Lyssa's family."

"But Miz Parnelli said there wasn't any."

"We have to check anyway. And we'll eventually have to notify social services, officially apply for temporary guardianship."

We? "Dan, that's a big undertaking."

"Yes."

Just like marrying her had been a big undertaking. He didn't have to say it. She read it in his eyes.

"I helped bring this child into the world. Lyssa entrusted her to me. They were her wishes. If by some chance this little girl has family, someone who's capable and wants to raise her, it'd be better to keep her here rather than put her in the system."

"You're right." Cryin' all night. She'd been married less than a month. A temporary wife, and now a temporary mother. What next? Where was it written that a woman should have everything but the kitchen sink thrown at her at once?

Lord have mercy, she needed to catch her breath.

"Let's take it a day at a time," he said. "Right now, we've got a baby to see to, and a funeral to prepare for."

THANK GOODNESS FOR NEIGHBORS—and for the speed of the grapevine.

Dan left her alone with the baby again while Vera Tillis opened up the General Store so he could purchase the essentials they would need.

A constant stream of neighbors—bringing a portable crib, a car seat, linens and clothes their children had outgrown—provided for the rest of Shayna's needs—and a few of Amy's as well.

She knew as much about babies as a cow did about ballet lessons. Via the expertise of all the new mothers in town, though, Amy received a crash course in mixing infant formula and changing diapers.

"Don't worry," Emily Bodine said. "Taking care of this little baby will come naturally."

"You're kidding, right? I feel about as far from natural as one can get."

Emily smiled. "Trust me. I've been in your shoes."

"I guess I should feel ashamed admitting my terror to a woman who handles twins."

"I gave birth to those twins, yes, but I had no idea what to do with them. I was a surrogate for my sister and brother-in-law—who happened to be Cheyenne's brother, as well. I was an ad executive with my mind made up that I was merely a nine-month incubator and wouldn't need to concern myself over motherhood. When my sister and her husband died, the responsibility for the babies was suddenly all mine. I didn't have a lick of experience. But Cheyenne was there for me. As Dan will be there for you. And if you need anything, anything at all, you've only to pick up the phone and give a holler and you'll have more ladies in your kitchen than you can count."

Emily eased the now sleeping baby into the portable crib Hannah Malone had brought over and assembled.

"I have awful fears of dropping her," she admitted.

Laughing softly, Emily patted Amy's arm. "You're talking to a certifiable klutz here, a woman who mows down entire displays of canned goods at the general store and can't back out of a parking space without having to fill out an accident report with her husband. You don't think I worried about the same thing?"

"So, I'm normal?"

"Absolutely. You'll be fine. The twins are about the same age as Shayna, three months, but they're a bit bigger. The clothes in the bag should fit fine—plenty of pink girly stuff. I don't think it'll hurt her femininity any to wear the blue ones, either. Just plunk a bow in her hair."

A bow. Amy didn't think she'd be tackling elaborate hairdos on this infant's nearly nonexistent fuzzy hair anytime soon. Diapers and snaps were going to be challenge enough.

"Well, I better get back to Cheyenne and see if

he's pulling his hair out yet. I left the twins at the sheriff's station with him and the deputies. The kids are teething and the guys are likely to lock them in a cell for bad behavior.''

Teething. Oh, no. Did that happen this soon? ''Thank you for coming by, Emily. I appreciate the help. Everyone's been so nice.''

''Anytime. That's what neighbors are for.''

Feeling like she'd fallen down the rabbit hole in an *Alice in Wonderland* adventure, Amy stared at the sleeping baby in the crib.

Oh, Shayna was a cutie. There was no doubting that.

But Amy hadn't been a child who played with dolls. She'd been focused on grand adventures. What did she know about teething and feeding schedules?

But determination would come through for her. Dan had lives depending on him all the time through the church, which meant this child's care would fall on her a good portion of the time.

Plus he was dealing with his grief over Lyssa's death.

Amy had never had anyone counting on her the way a helpless infant no doubt would. Watching over her mother sort of fell in the same category, but it was different.

Thinking of her mother, though, reminded her that Dan had helped her out. And now he needed her help in return.

She'd dedicated three months to this agreement.

Adjusting the quilt over the sleeping baby, Amy decided to make the best of it.

THEY HAD THE FUNERAL the next day. Clouds billowed overhead, promising snow, but as Dan said his final words, a ray of buttery sunshine found an opening and shone down on the cemetery.

Dan liked to believe that was God's way of letting them know that Lyssa was watching from heaven.

Because Lyssa had indeed been a ray of sunshine who'd kept her faith and searched for the good in everything and everyone when most people would have crawled into a hole and excused their dysfunction on a series of crummy breaks.

He thought about other funerals he'd spoken over. The hardest ones were the young ones—like Lyssa— who still had so much life ahead of them. Or the babies, like the LaBoard's premature daughter he'd buried in this same cemetery. They'd had such high hopes for beginning a family, yet instead of tucking their child into a crib and winding up a dancing mobile, they'd had to close the lid on a tiny white coffin.

In times of death, some family members left behind drew on faith, others shunned it in their pain.

In Lyssa's case, there was no one here who cared enough one way or the other.

A couple of her neighbors from the trailer park came. The rest of the people standing at the gravesite were his own friends and neighbors, here to support him and Amy.

He noted that Kelly Hammond was cuddling Shayna, the child wrapped in a thick blanket against the wind. Amy stood at her shoulder, looking tired after a near sleepless night with a new baby and grateful for the help.

She certainly hadn't signed on for this latest turn of events. At least Dan knew they'd get help from his friends. In this town, there were plenty of loving arms ready and willing to help out.

Still, the responsibility was primarily his. A child had been orphaned, left motherless.

And he'd been appointed the white knight.

That seemed to be happening to him a lot lately, as though he was being tested to see what it would take for him to go back on the vow he'd made fourteen years ago to never turn his back on someone in need.

So far, he was keeping his end of the bargain. But in doing so, he'd dragged Amy into it, as well.

AMY DIDN'T ALWAYS BOTHER with makeup, but at least she washed her face. She hadn't even found time for that simple ritual.

She could remember drink orders from four tables, recite them accurately to the bartender and deliver them back in front of the correct customer without missing a beat. In the past three days, she couldn't even remember where she put her hairbrush, or what time it had been when she'd fed the baby last.

Was she overfeeding the poor thing? Starving it. The baby cried and cried. Incessantly.

She hugged the warm little body to her chest. "I know, I know. You've lost your mama and that gives you every right in the world to caterwaul like a heartbroken kitty cat. I'm a poor substitute, baby doll, but I'm the best you've got right now." She glanced up.

"Ignore that. The better half of the substitution just walked in."

Dan smiled. "Rough day?"

"Emily said her babies are teething at three months. Maybe that's what's wrong here. I'm at my wits' end. Do you think we should call the doctor? I never knew a child could cry this consistently. It can't be healthy for her."

"Want me to have a go at it?"

"Shayna would probably appreciate it. I don't think she's used to me yet."

Dan took the baby, and she hushed in a matter of minutes.

"Well, that's a bit demoralizing."

"She probably just senses that you're tired."

"Or she recognizes you. You've been in her life since she was born. Do you think she knows her mother is gone?"

Sadness swept his face and she was sorry she'd brought up the grief. "Maybe. But I think she knows she's safe with us. Babies adapt pretty quickly."

"Can you define 'pretty quickly' for me?"

He chuckled. "If you want to go on to bed, I'll take it from here."

She sighed. He'd put in a full day of working. He was as tired as she was.

"No. If you'll take over with her for a bit, though, I'll see if I can wade through the mess in the kitchen. It looks like a spoiled Pekingese tore through there with malicious intent."

"That bad?"

"Worse. How do people keep up with housekeeping and personal hygiene. I've probably got yesterday's makeup under my eyes and if my hair's seen a brush in the past two days, nobody's told me about it. It's a wonder you didn't scream and run right back out the door when you got a good gander at me.''

''I'm not a screamer.''

She opened her mouth, lewd thoughts running through her head. Honestly. Sex should have been the last thing on her mind. She was so tired she didn't think she'd have enough energy to return a kiss, much less engage in the kind of activity that would result in screaming.

Not that she, herself, was a screamer. She didn't think.

''Um, I'll just…go stick my hands in a sink of dishwater.''

The sound of his soft chuckle followed her out of the room. Okay, she was tired. She'd give herself a break there. But that was no excuse for letting her mind trip off into forbidden territory.

It was just that he looked so darn good. After spending an entire day trying to second-guess the needs of a child with absolutely no verbal skills—but plenty of stinky bad habits—it stood to reason she'd react to a sexy cowboy preacher whose hat nearly scraped the top of the doorway when he walked into the room, and whose come-and-get-me chocolate-brown eyes had alighted on her like she was Miss Georgia in the swimsuit competition.

And Lord, how he looked when he held that tiny baby girl in his massive arms, his smile gentle, his hat tipped low over his brow. Now if *that* wasn't enough to stir a woman's heart, then the woman in question simply didn't possess one.

Honestly.

She rinsed bottles, loaded the dishwasher and wiped down the counters. Opening the kitchen door, she stepped out on the porch with an open milk carton she'd used to save scraps in for the stray cat she'd been feeding, and nearly shrieked when she encountered a raccoon helping himself to the dish she'd set out for the cat.

"Scat," she admonished, and stamped her foot. "I'm not feeding you, too." As though she had any control. She should have known stray cats weren't the only varmints looking for a free meal. "Here, kitty, kitty."

A bushy gray cat with a torn ear jumped nimbly up on the porch, keeping his distance, tail swishing.

"If I'm going to put myself out to feed you, the least you could do is show up for dinner and eat it before the rest of the animal kingdom gets wind and starts hanging around my door." She dumped scraps into the metal bowl.

"I don't know why I'm doing this for you," she muttered. "Every time I turn around these past three days, I'm feeding somebody who doesn't even have the verbal skills to carry on a conversation with me. How do I even know if you like what I'm giving you? And why the hell am I talking to a cat, anyway?"

Worried that she might hear a clap of thunder overhead because of uttering a cuss word on the steps of the rectory, she stepped back inside, gave a longing look at the open door of her dark room, then shut off the kitchen light and slipped into the bathroom to run a washcloth over her face—both to revive herself and to restore some order to her appearance.

No telling if Shayna would wake from her catnap in Dan's arms and it would be her turn again. No sense scaring the child with raccoon circles under her eyes. Maybe that's what was the matter, the reason the baby cried so much. Her substitute mother was scaring the daylights out of her.

When she walked back into the living room, Dan was adding logs to the fire, his hat resting on the end table, his boots lying next to the ottoman.

"Where's the baby?"

"I put her to bed."

Amy sighed. "Just like that? Do you think she'll stay down?"

"She seemed pretty worn-out."

She flopped down on the couch and drew up her knees. "I'm not doing so great, am I?"

"Why do you say that?"

"The poor thing wears herself out crying and I don't have the skills to comfort her."

He set down the poker and sat next to her on the sofa, leather creaking under denim. "You're doing great, Amy. And I appreciate it."

She nodded. Actually, she was overstating a bit. Shayna hadn't cried *all* day. It just felt like it. There had been moments of joy in amongst the nerves, moments when the sweet child had smiled and cooed and curled trustingly into her chest.

Not many of those moments, mind you, but they were there.

She looked at Dan's handsome face, firelight reflecting off the highlights in his hair.

"What makes you do this?"

"What?"

"Marry a stranger without thought. Take in a baby without an argument."

"I *did* give the marriage some thought, and who was there to argue with about the child?"

"You know what I'm talking about."

He eased back against the couch. "After my wild days of youth, I got into a bit of trouble and finally decided I needed to settle down. My behavior was causing a lot of pressure on my family, though I've got to say, they never held it over my head, never threatened to kick me out or lectured me about keeping up appearances because of who my father was. That unconditional love and acceptance hit me one day, made me realize how lucky I was and what a screw-up I'd become."

She listened as he told her about going back to college, copping out when his buddies needed a designated driver.

"I'd turned over a new leaf, was full of my own righteousness, judging their behavior. It didn't matter that I'd been one of the biggest party hounds before. I stood rigidly by my newfound morals and told the guys I had an exam to study for."

He glanced away at the fire. "The call came into the dorm around 2:00 a.m. There'd been an alcohol-related accident. One person was dead at the scene, another critically injured. I could have prevented that tragedy, but I'd turned my back on my friends because I didn't approve, because it didn't go along with what I felt was right. I'd elevated myself above them, judged them."

"Oh, Dan."

"Chad's spine was severed and the doctors said he'd never walk again. As I stood over his hospital bed, held his hand as he wept over the news of having to live the rest of his life in a wheelchair, I made a vow never again to turn my back on a person in need."

And because of that incident, that vow, he'd been unable—or unwilling—to deny her when she'd sought him out with her marriage proposal.

At last, she understood the depth of the pressure he must have been feeling, knowing if he turned her down, she and her mother would lose their family home.

Similar to the guilt he carried over his friend losing the use of his legs.

And then there was the baby. He hadn't turned his back on Shayna, because the child would end up in the system. Oh, sure, a family would adopt a baby in a snap, but there were no guarantees that the home would be stable, that the child would be safe.

And because of the horrors he'd alluded to of what Lyssa had suffered as a child, safety would be a paramount issue.

Lyssa had asked for his promise.

He'd given it the moment he'd taken the baby from Ellen Parnelli's arms.

Chapter Nine

Understanding him better now, Amy looked at him through new eyes. He was trustworthy. Capable. He should have been married to the love of his life and had a house full of contented kids.

She didn't let herself examine the little pang that jolted her when she subconsciously cast herself in the role of his soul mate, imagining the joys of helping him produce those happy kids.

It was merely the image of seeing him with Shayna, she told herself. Those strong, loving hands holding a helpless child.

"You're good father material," she said.

"Thanks for the vote of confidence. Frankly, I'm developing more respect for how Daniel felt when he was tossed to the lions."

She chuckled and patted his arm. She was getting used to him speaking in or relating to parables. "Shayna doesn't have teeth yet."

"That you know of."

"True." She let her gaze travel over his handsome face, his flat stomach where his shirt tucked into his belted jeans. The man was a prime catch.

"You mentioned that most women are scared off by your vocation. Aside from the occasional date, have you ever been in a long-term relationship?"

He shifted his head against the back of the couch, looked at her and grinned. "You want to know if I've had sex, don't you?"

"Would you stop that! Talk about *me* being obsessed by sex."

"Are you?"

"*You're* the one who keeps reading stuff into perfectly innocent questions. Honestly. If you don't want to answer, then don't."

"Oh, I don't mind answering." He straightened on the sofa, turned toward her. "I've a feeling you've still got me up on somewhat of a pedestal. I'm about to fall off it. My first sexual encounter was with an older woman. I was sixteen, she was twenty-three. I was...fairly grateful for the experience."

She didn't know whether to laugh or be scandalized. "Shame on her. You were jailbait. And a minister's son!"

"And a perfectly normal, hormone-crazed teenage boy. I went through a period of time where I didn't practice a great deal of discretion."

"I see."

"Surprise you?"

"Not really. I guess I can imagine some of your antics after hearing about your drunken ride down Main Street on a borrowed tractor."

"Now, who told you about that?"

She laughed at his mock outrage. "Cheyenne Bodine, I think. Or it might have been the doctor. I found myself in the middle of a bunch of your buddies the other day after church. They seemed happy enough to give me a bit of the down and dirty on you.''

''Payback.''

''For what?''

''I sort of helped along a few rumors when several of them were dating their wives.''

''You broke a confidence?''

''No. The confidence wasn't told to me. I got it secondhand, and nobody said it was a secret, so I helped spread the word about pending nuptials and such.''

''Ah, aiding and abetting the matchmakers, were you?''

''Something like that.''

She curled her legs under her and turned on the couch to more fully face him, sinking comfortably into the soft leather.

''So, what about your own love life?'' she asked.

''I fell in love once, when I first started my ministry. The relationship didn't stand up to the demands my job put on my time. Glenda said I gave away a piece of myself to everyone else and there wasn't enough left over for her.''

''I'm sorry. I know how that feels. I got dumped for the same reason. I dated an insurance guy for two years, and I thought we were headed for marriage, convinced myself that if we exchanged rings he'd change his mind and come see the world with me. He conducted most of his work from a cell phone and laptop computer, so it wasn't like he had any firm ties to the town or anything. Instead, he was boinking half the girls in the country club every time I took an out-of-town assignment with the newspaper, or got a lead on a photography gig.''

"The guy must have been an idiot."

"Thank you." She reached out and brushed his arm with her fingertips for aligning himself as an ally. "I caught him red-handed when I came home early one day, and the jerk blamed *me* because he couldn't keep his pants zipped."

"You didn't believe him, did you?"

She shrugged. "It sticks in the back of my mind. I haven't had a relationship since, haven't put it to the test. I know where I want to go with my career. And Doyle showed me that my dream doesn't mix with a happily-ever-after commitment."

"So, you don't want that? Happily-ever-after?"

"Someday, sure. I want my big break first."

"And you believe *National Geographic* will be that break?"

"It could be. It's hard to say. The events of the past months prove that none of us has any way of knowing what's around the corner. But it's what I want. And I believe I have the determination to stick to it until I make it."

"With that positive attitude, I'm sure you will." He gave her hand a squeeze, got up and adjusted the screen in front of the fire. "I'm thinking it's about time we went to bed. What do you say?"

Her heart lurched into her throat. *For pity's sake, Amy.* He didn't mean go to bed *together*.

She stood and took the hand he held out to her. Roommates, she reminded herself. Thrown together by circumstances neither of them had asked for or could control.

MILDRED AND OPAL ARRIVED early the next morning. Amy was staring at the coffeepot, wishing it would hurry up and drip, thinking she'd be better off mainlining it straight into a vein. She was so tired she could curl up and sleep for a week.

Good manners had her reluctantly tearing herself away from the dripping pot and going to greet the visitors Dan had already opened the door to.

The ladies dropped their matching patent-leather pocketbooks, set down a covered casserole dish and launched into a race to see who could unbutton her wool coat the fastest and get her hands on the baby.

Mildred won by cheating, leaving her coat hanging open and snatching the baby right out of Dan's arms. "Oh, here's the little lamb. Bless her heart. Isn't she just precious, sister?"

Opal folded her coat over a nearby chair and came to stand over Mildred's shoulder. "Yes. So sad to lose a mother at this young age."

"Good morning to you, ladies," Dan said dryly.

Mildred and Opal barely gave him a glance. Amy grinned. In this town, when there was a baby around, adults might as well be invisible.

"Y'all are out early," Amy said, coming into the room.

"Oh, love," Opal said. "How are you holding up?"

"By a thread," she said with a laugh.

Dan raised a brow. "I notice nobody thought to ask how *I'm* holding up."

Mildred laughed. "Just like a man. Hates to be left out."

"Sister," Opal admonished. "Don't insult the pastor in his own home. And stop hogging that child."

"Since I appear to be expendable, I've got some phone calls to make. Will you ladies excuse me?"

Opal waved him off with a flick of her hand, cooing to the baby that Mildred had reluctantly relinquished into her arms.

Amy grinned at his affronted expression. Actually, there was relief there, too. He was beat, had been up as many times during the night as she had.

"I've got a pot of coffee brewing," she said to him. "Do you want me to bring you a cup?"

"I'm good for now. I had some earlier."

"Yeah, and thanks for leaving the pot empty."

"Sorry. I got sidetracked."

She smiled to let him know she was kidding. Since she couldn't even find time to brush her hair half the time, she understood how a crying baby would preempt brewing a second pot of coffee.

"How about you two," she said to Mildred and Opal when Dan left to go into his study. "Will you join me in the kitchen for a shot of caffeine? I confess, I'm about to have a fit if I don't get a little pep."

Mildred picked up the casserole dish and another plate Amy hadn't noticed. "Can't have folks having a fit in the middle of the living room. Sister and I brought scones. That'll pep you right up. Eden Stratton makes them and you'll think you've died and gone to heaven."

"Bless you. I'm starving. Seems like all I do is feed babies and stray animals on the back porch, but I don't have enough hands or time to feed myself."

"Well, we can't have you wasting away to nothing. You'll make yourself sick. You just sit right down," Mildred said, bustling around the kitchen, "and let us do for you."

"I can—"

"Hush now," Opal said, easily setting out cups and arranging scones on a plate while Mildred poured coffee and put the casserole in the refrigerator. Awed, Amy watched the ladies take charge of the kitchen, miraculously restoring order, Opal never missing a beat even though she was holding the baby in one arm.

Amazing. Amy needed two hands to accomplish things. Which was why nothing seemed to be getting accomplished.

Feeling relieved that there were capable, grand-motherly types to run the show for a while, she took a much-needed sip of coffee and bit into a fluffy scone that melted in her mouth and made her close her eyes on a moan.

"Told you they were fabulous, didn't I?"

"Better than fabulous. The woman's a genius."

"That she is. Gave up her catering business in Texas and made her home here. Now, we're reaping the rewards—and expanding our waistlines to boot."

"Eden gave up her business?"

"Dreams have a way of changing. Love will do that."

Both Mildred and Opal gave Amy a quick, knowing look. Uh-oh. Were they part of the matchmaking circle she'd heard so much about?

Mildred took the baby back from Opal and sat down at the kitchen table across from Amy, leaving Opal staring, obviously wondering how her sister had maneuvered the slick switch. With a huff, she sat down as well.

"So, tell us," Mildred said. "How is the new marriage working out? Must put a bit of a crimp in things with the baby and all."

"You know it's not that kind of a marriage," Amy objected. The widows knew about the will, about the jeopardy of losing her mother's home and the coveted job pending.

"Don't pay any mind to Mildred," Opal said. "She's gone all moon-eyed over the judge and her feeble brain's stuck in a groove."

"Wouldn't do your stodgy brain any harm to open up to a little romance. Henry Jenkins over at the Feed and Seed would be more than happy to talk you out of your panties if you'd get your nose out of the air long enough to take a good look."

"Honestly, Mildred. Mind your language. There's a child present." Opal patted her military-short gray hair, then sloshed coffee when she snatched up her cup. "Oh, now you've made me make a mess."

"You see what I put up with?" Mildred said to Amy. "Blames me for everything. I keep telling her if she'd have a little sex she'd get down off her high horse and feel better in the bargain."

Amy nearly spewed her coffee across the table.

"Mildred! Really! Shush before Pastor Dan comes in and hears you speaking in such an unseemly manner."

Mildred grinned. "She's such a prude."

Amy wasn't sure what to say to that.

Opal glared at Mildred, then attempted to change the subject. "What do you hear from your mother, dear?"

"I've been so busy since we got Shayna that I haven't called her." And she felt guilty for that. Chandra wasn't one to be on her own easily.

"I'm sure she'll understand when you explain it to her," Mildred said. "You're a wonderful daughter for sacrificing for your mother this way—not that marriage to Dan Lucas is a sacrifice, mind you. The man is a hunk."

"Yes, well..." *Hmm.*

Dan came into the room and Amy's gaze darted to his. Had he heard Mildred calling him a hunk?

He winked at her, snagged a scone off the plate and poured himself a cup of coffee. "Always nice to know I've got neighbors in my corner expounding on my attributes."

Amy groaned and watched him sashay back out of the room.

"We shouldn't encourage his ego."

"Oh, I don't know about that. Sister and I are always happy to help out where love's involved."

"It's not—"

"We must be going, dear." Mildred plopped Shayna in Amy's arms and fairly dragged Opal to her feet.

Stunned, Amy watched them bustle out of the house. They knew good and well that this was a mere marriage of convenience, but the Bagley widows were apparently rooting for a change in the rules.

THE WIDOWS HADN'T BEEN GONE long when a rusty old pickup pulled up at the back door.

Jenny White Cloud got out, carrying a large sack. Nothing like a new baby to bring out a string of company.

Generally, Amy considered herself a private person, enjoyed solitude. However, with her life in an uproar and the added responsibilities, she was happy and *relieved* with all the visitors.

She opened the door, smiling. "Jenny. It's good to see you again. I'm glad you stopped by. I have something for you. Come in."

"I can only stay a minute. I have brought a gift for the child."

"You didn't have to do that."

"Of course not." From the bag, she removed a woven blanket.

"Oh, that's the one I was working on, isn't it?"

"Yes. It turned out nice, didn't it? When we heard about the child, we altered the dimensions so it would be suitable for the babe. It is a good thing that you and Pastor Dan have done. Taking in this child. And the blanket, made partially with your own hands will be a gift the child can pass on to her own children."

Amy felt a pang. She wouldn't be here long enough for a handmade blanket to carry valued memories. Besides, she'd only woven a couple of rows. The rest of the ladies had designed the pattern and done the beautiful work.

"You know, among our people, we believe that there are no orphans—regardless of race—nor the need for courts and such. We take care of our own. It is good to see others adopting our ways."

"Your nephew, Cheyenne Bodine, is still searching to see if Shayna has family that we don't know about."

Amy caught herself hoping he wouldn't be successful. She looked at the blond-headed, blue-eyed baby. She was a handful, but she was crying less now, adapting. The thought of uprooting her again, having to get used to more strange people, no telling how many more times, was unthinkable.

Amy's own life had never been touched with these problems. Sure, she'd been independent and made her own money, but the underlying security was there. Her family had wealth that Shayna's hadn't. Poverty had made this child vulnerable.

Even if she wasn't around to see to it, Dan would make sure this child prospered. He'd made a promise. She knew him well enough to know he wouldn't ever go back on that promise.

"I have something for you, as well." With the baby in her arms she hesitated.

"Here, I would love to hold the child," Jenny said.

"Thanks. I haven't gotten the hang of doing two things at once. Seems I'm a person who needs two hands to clap. I'll be right back. I want to let Dan know you're here. He'll want to thank you for the gift, too.''

She went to her darkroom and grabbed a folder with photos she'd managed to process in between Shayna's naps. She couldn't find time to match her socks, but she developed film. The process soothed her. In this room, she lost herself in the wonder of images that appeared on glossy paper, images she often didn't even remember capturing.

''Have a look at these,'' she said, putting the folder on the kitchen table, then tearing out of the room to call Dan.

Sitting at his desk in the study, he lifted his head when she knocked on the door.

''My turn with the baby?'' he asked.

''No. Jenny White Cloud is here. She brought Shayna a gift. I thought maybe you'd want to say hello.''

He smiled. ''Thanks. I'd like that.''

He followed her out of the room, then put a hand on her shoulder, stopping her. She felt his wide palm brush at her backside and jumped.

He grinned. ''You had powder on your butt.''

''Oh. Thank you. I spilled the formula mix. I'd thought I got it all wiped up.''

''Evidently you did. Just not in the traditional way.''

''I'm a mess, aren't I?''

''You'll hit your stride.''

Yes, well, she was going to pay better attention from now on. Her husband *was* a hunk. Having a baby in the house hadn't caused him to let his appearance go to the dogs.

"Hey, Jenny," he said, bending down to give the small woman a hug.

"Pastor. It is good to see you. I only stopped by to deliver the blanket your wife made."

"I didn't make it," Amy objected.

"When we weave a group blanket, it has the name of all the weavers. Your hands helped in the creation so the fabric bears part of your soul. It will be a treasure in your family, and for the children you wrap in it. They will feel your spirit of love and comfort."

She looked at Dan, wondered how he felt about Jenny's words. He knew she wouldn't be here long enough for her contribution to a blanket to be considered a treasure. Shayna would probably never even remember her.

He glanced away and looked at the photographs spread out in front of Jenny. "These are excellent."

"Yes, I do not think I can accept them. You will want to save them for yourself, Amy. At least this one," Jenny said, pointing to the photo of the circle of ladies weaving the blanket. "It shows your blanket."

"I have a double print," Amy admitted. "These are my gift to you."

"In that case, I thank you. These are my sister's children playing in the street," she said, pointing to the little girls playing hopscotch. "And this one is the husband of my cousin. My cousin is no longer with us, and Joe Little Coyote pines for her. He is our medicine man, and he lost faith in his powers when he could not heal his wife. He has given up hope.''

It was the photo of the man sitting on the porch.

"I'm working on restoring that," Dan said.

"If anyone can, it will be you, Pastor Dan." Jenny stood and transferred the baby to him. "I have one more gift." From the bag, she withdrew a fabric back-pack-type sling, which she slipped over Amy's head and adjusted against her chest.

"It is for the baby, so you may have your two hands free...to clap if you wish," she said with a smile.

"Perfect," Dan said. "Emily has one of these for the twins. Will it fit me, too?"

"Of course."

"Now, don't be coveting my gift," Amy said. "You're more adept than I am at doing things one-handed. Give me the baby. Let's try it out."

Shayna, obviously happy at being passed around like a doll and the center of attention, waved her arms and kicked her legs, blowing spit bubbles. It took all three of them to wrestle the child into the sling.

"She can ride facing forward or toward your chest, however you feel comfortable," Jenny said.

"She likes to see where she's going, so let's try it facing forward first."

With holes for her legs and arms, the baby was perfectly supported. Still Amy wrapped an arm across the baby's stomach for added security.

Dan adjusted the straps over her shoulders, his knuckles brushing her breasts. It couldn't be helped.

Her gaze darted to his, then away. No sense calling

attention to such a minor slip—even though she'd been extraordinarily aware of his touch.

He stepped back and made googly faces at the baby, who kicked her feet against Amy's stomach.

"Hey, she's smiling. I think she likes it."

Amy tried to crane her neck to see the smile for herself. "Are you sure?"

"I'm looking at her. I'm sure. Try it with no hands."

"What if she slips out or something. She's quite a wiggle worm."

"She will not slip," Jenny said.

Slowly, reluctantly, Amy took her hand away. The child hung down the front of her and stayed put. "It worked."

"Did you expect her to end up on the floor?" Dan asked.

"If you recall, I've seen the results of that type of accident."

"There will be no accidents," Jenny said. "You have a maternal gift."

Amy didn't think that was so but didn't argue.

"Thank you for the gifts, Jenny," Amy said.

"And thank you. You are welcome in our home anytime. We will make more blankets."

"I'd like that."

When Jenny gathered up her purse, Dan walked her out to the car.

"Okay, Shayna. I'm going to take a step. Hold on tight." As an extra precaution, she put her arm back around the baby and took a few steps. So far so good. Carefully she let go and took another step.

"Hey, this is pretty slick. You can help me wash the dishes. No, wait. That's no fun. We'll teach you to develop pictures. You might get a little scared when I have to turn off the light, but it'll be okay. I'll be right there with you, and it'll only be for a couple of minutes. I have to root around like a raccoon in the dark so I don't expose the film, but I'm pretty good, and I'm quick about it. And I bet you'll like the red light in there. It's very pretty. On second thought, we better start out with easy stuff. You're a bit little yet to breathe chemical fumes."

She turned and saw Dan leaning against the doorjamb, watching her, grinning.

"Planning to make her a student of photography?"

She shrugged. "Teach them while they're young."

He pushed away from the wall and crossed the room, his steps slow and measured, his gaze on hers. Spellbound, she couldn't take her eyes from him.

Her heart pounded. He was a joy to watch, tall and strong, masculine and sexy. The way he looked at a woman...well, it was exciting. Doubly exciting that the woman he was looking at was her.

When he stopped within inches of her, his gaze shifted to the baby at her chest.

She let out a breath. Why in the world had she thought he was coming across the room to kiss her?

Honestly. The man shouldn't give off those sexy pheromones if he didn't mean business.

And she shouldn't be thinking about that kind of business in the first place. She owed him more than she could ever repay. Encouraging seduction, on either of their parts, carried too high a price. The price of Dan's moral conscience—and her own.

Chapter Ten

On Valentine's Day, Amy had been a wife for a month and a mother for two weeks. She was adapting to the second pretty well, but the jury was still out on the first.

The attraction between her and Dan was heating up. It was getting harder by the day to remember the terms of the marriage, to remember the hands-off policy.

She was having dreams, vivid dreams, about him very definitely putting his hands on her, and vice versa.

Picking up the phone, she dialed her mother's telephone number. She needed to remind herself why she was here. And she needed to make sure her mom was okay.

When Chandra breathlessly answered after the eighth ring, Amy frowned.

"Mom. It's me. Are you all right?"

"Oh, Amy, it's lovely to hear your voice. Yes, I'm fine."

"You sound out of breath."

Chandra giggled. Amy blinked. Her mother, terribly shy, normally didn't *giggle*. She was soft-spoken, tentative, rarely animated.

"I've just walked in the door and had to run a bit."

"Were you in the garden, then?" Chandra found solace among her flowers. They were her friends—those happy pansies and showy hydrangeas. Gramps had built a greenhouse for her so she could have exotic blooms year-round regardless of the weather.

"Close. I ran over to Hugh Webster's nursery. My sweet peas were wilting—a fungus, I'd suspected. That man has a way with plants that just makes me want to sigh. He offered me a job, Amy. Can you imagine. I'm a working woman now."

Amy sat right down in the closest chair. A job? Her mother?

"Hugh says I've magic in my hands. Imagine that." She giggled again, the sound breathy. With her mouth hanging open, Amy listened as her mother rattled on, exclaiming over "Hugh this" and "Hugh that," bouncing back and forth between flowers and the sensuality of earth beneath her "magic" hands and the battery she'd had Zeke at the local garage replace in the Impala.

Her *mother* had gone to a repair garage and had the battery replaced? On her own? Amy looked at the calendar, touched the tile countertop, assuring herself she was awake and hadn't slipped into somebody else's dream.

"Zeke says the Impala's in good shape—which is thanks to your grandfather for taking it in regularly for service. You would have been proud of me, Amy, for doing this on my own. Of course, Hugh had a hand in it. He gave me a pep talk, made me feel so…oh, dear. Here comes Maisy Laird. She's such a busybody. She'll want to know why I've gone to work after all these years. Gossips. They make me weary.'' She took a breath. ''You're doing fine, hon?''

''Yes.'' She barely got the word out before Chandra started talking again.

''Of course you are. You're always fine. I must run. Maisy's pinching my azaleas. She'll have the bush plucked bare if I don't stop her. Call me soon. If I'm not here, you can reach me at Hugh's. I love you, hon. Bye.''

Somewhat dazed, Amy hung up the phone. Since Shayna was still napping, she decided to work out her confusion in the darkroom.

Interesting that Chandra hadn't asked about Amy's marriage, hadn't been all fluttery and nervous about the precarious state of her home's stability.

It had only been a month, yet without Amy there to take care of her, Mom had gotten a job. And changed the battery in the car. And appeared smitten with Hugh Webster.

There had been something in Chandra's voice, an excitement. Over getting a job for the first time in her life? Or the man?

Amy wasn't sure how she felt about her mother having a relationship with another man, replacing her dad.

She was trying so hard to prove that her dad's choices were good ones. To make his life count. If

Mom fell in love with someone else, another piece of Dad would fade away.

And with her mother's obvious newfound strength in getting a job, why was Amy here? Married to a man who surely wouldn't have married her had there been other choices.

Had she and Gramps been keeping Chandra dependent? Had she encouraged the very thing she found abhorrent?

Neediness?

Since she was only sorting through contact sheets, she hadn't closed the door. Although she had a baby monitor to listen for Shayna's cries, she still felt better relying on her own hearing.

A soft knock on the doorjamb had her turning around.

Dan stood there, looking like a man who'd come courting. In one hand, he held a huge stuffed animal; in the other, a bouquet of red roses. On his face was an expression of masculine pride.

"Happy Valentine's Day," he said, and handed her the bouquet, setting the floppy teddy bear on the low counter by the washing machine. "The bear's for Shayna. I know it's a little big, but I figure she'll grow into it."

The man was obviously a romantic.

Interesting that she'd just been talking to her mother about flowers, and nurseries—and the man who ran one.

Touched, Amy buried her nose in the roses. "Thank you. I've never received flowers from a man before."

"You're joking."

"No. I'm not the type of woman who inspires them."

"You're exactly the type of woman who inspires them. Look at you."

Yes, look at her. She'd brushed her hair and put on a little makeup, but she was wearing her usual attire of ancient jeans and one of her father's old shirts hanging open over a T-shirt decorated with baby spit-up.

"I think we need to get you some spectacles, Pastor. You've obviously spent too many nights reading under poor light and have ruined your eyesight."

She turned and took down a vase from the overhead cabinet, filled it with water and arranged her roses. In her nervousness, she didn't take the time to slice the ends off under running water like she'd been taught. Her mother would have tsked.

She smelled the subtle scent of his sandalwood cologne as he moved behind her, crowding her, the scent vying with the smell of processing chemicals and the heady aroma of the flowers.

Honestly. This room was her sanctuary. And Dan's presence in it made her as nervous as a fly in a glue jar.

"What are you working on?"

"Nothing much."

Dan shifted through the glossy photos in an open folder. Pictures of Shayna, ones of him holding the baby, Mildred and Opal faced off in battle, underlying smirks on their faces.

Each time he was confronted with her work, he was

amazed. She took the ordinary and made it appear spectacular, forever finding the emotional angles in her shots: a lone wolf in the snow with his nose raised to catch a scent; a young buck poised by the frozen stream; their neighbors gazing at their children or spouses with unadulterated love that was nearly palpable; the laughter and tears of the young and old.

She had talent. A gift. He recalled her impassioned words about her determination to succeed.

He had no doubt she would. And that very knowledge gave him a punch in the gut. He admired her goals but selfishly lamented what that meant for them, was reminded that she wasn't his to hold.

And more and more lately, he wanted to hold her.

He looked down at her, caught her staring at his mouth. Emotions sizzled. For the time being, she was his wife. Today was the day to celebrate lovers.

And he was a man with a powerful thirst.

He touched the smooth alabaster skin of her face, traced the outline of her full lower lip.

"Dan," she warned, but her voice didn't hold any punch.

"Amy," he countered, and lowered his head. She smelled of baby powder and processing chemicals.

Her sigh of surrender set off something inside him, her tentative touch against his chest inflaming him. Backing her against the counter, he deepened the kiss, dived into the sweet taste of her like a starving man at a feast. He had a thought that he should slow down, that he shouldn't be leading them down this road, but his desire was too huge, the responsive woman beneath his hands too tempting.

Amy wrapped her arms around his neck and held on for dear life. This was exactly what she needed, exactly what she wanted. He made her feel like the sexiest woman on the planet, drew her out.

The buckle of his belt pressed into her stomach, the hard ridge of his arousal against her pubic bone intoxicating her.

Static from the baby monitor on the counter beside them brought her back to earth. Shayna fussed, then gave a coughing little cry.

Amy sighed and eased her hold on his shoulders, resting her forehead against his.

Saved by the baby.

She didn't know whether to be relieved or to curse.

She was so torn. Torn between the desire in her heart and the passion in her soul.

Desire for her temporary husband, and passion for her career dreams.

"I'll go get her," Dan said.

She nodded.

He paused at the door. "Amy?"

She looked up.

"This isn't finished."

It was a warning. Or a promise.

Oh, dear Lord. What now?

WHEN DORA CALLAHAN STOPPED by several days later, Amy was glad of the company. She was walking on eggshells around her husband, in a state of sexual vacillation. Thank goodness, his busy schedule and Shayna's demands kept them apart. Otherwise, she might have thrown caution to the wind and instigated something they'd both be sorry for.

Still her mind was consumed with images of that kiss, of what might have happened if Shayna's cries hadn't interrupted them.

"I was over at Tillis's," Dora said, "and the ladies snagged my kids, so I thought I'd pop over and see how you're getting along."

"Surviving. You were right, it's getting a little easier. Shayna's napping more now, developing a bit of a schedule, though she's still not sleeping through the night. Thanks for the tip about teething. Nothing's broken through the skin yet, and she fights the gel I put on her gums, but she gnaws like a toothless beaver on the teething ring. I keep it in the fridge and she seems to like the cold—which gave Dan the bright idea of sharing his Popsicle with her the other day." Her tone was dry and disapproving. It struck her that she sounded just like a mother.

"Men," Dora said with a laugh. "A little lick won't hurt her, though." She glanced toward the open door of Amy's darkroom. "I'm going to be tacky and ask if you'll let me see your setup in there."

"Nothing tacky about it. I love to show off my lab."

"And I love listening to your accent. Makes me want to keep you talking. You and Eden Stratton sound so much alike, but different in small ways. Eden's from Texas. You're Georgia, right?"

"Yes."

"That must be the difference. Still, it tickles me."

Amy grinned and opened the door to the lab. "We aim to please."

Dora exclaimed over all the fancy equipment and paged through the photographs lying about. "These are brilliant. I'm almost ashamed to ask to see the ones I took of your wedding."

"Oh, stop." She took out the contact sheet of the thumbnail prints and handed it to Dora.

"You didn't develop any?"

Amy hesitated, then retrieved a binder out of the cupboard.

"Come on. Hand it over." Dora snagged the binder and opened it. There was only one picture in it.

"Oh, my. This is fabulous, even if I do say so myself. Very telling."

Amy sighed. "I thought what I was feeling was a fluke until I looked at this photo."

"And what is it that you're feeling?"

She needed to confide in someone. "I'm having lusty thoughts about my husband and I'm ashamed of myself."

Dora, tongue in cheek, said, "Did I ever mention that my father's a minister?"

Amy raised her brows. "No. You know I'm starting to get annoyed how all you holy people walk around masquerading as normal folks."

Dora nearly fell out laughing. "You sound like my husband. When I came to Shotgun Ridge, Ethan was up on the stage being auctioned off as a bachelor for charity. He was the town playboy and I'd come to deliver his baby daughter to him—Katie. You see, his past had come back to bite him in the rear. When he found out who my father was, he was scared to death of me, treated me like a nun. So, I asked Hannah Malone for some tips and set about to seduce him.''

''I can't seduce Dan!''

''Why not? You're married to him.''

''Exactly. And if we act on this…this…whatever it is, it'll ruin his chance for an annulment.''

''Do you plan to announce it to the world if you consummate your marriage?''

''No.''

Dora shrugged as if to say, ''There you go.''

Instead of helping, Amy was more confused than ever.

LATER THAT EVENING, Amy came downstairs on her way to the darkroom. Shayna was in bed for the night and she wasn't sure where Dan was.

The house was quiet, except for a particularly vicious wind batting at the windows.

A little boy with a mop of curly red hair and freckles who looked to be around eight years old sat in the corner of the living room, playing with the toys.

She glanced at the study door, which was partially open. A couple sat huddled together on the sofa by Dan's desk.

She looked back at the little boy. So this is why Dan kept toys in his house.

''Hi,'' she said, hesitating inside the room, not sure if she should leave him be. When the boy looked up, the fear and entreaty in his wide blue eyes drew her in. ''I'm Amy. What's your name?''

"Jeremy. My mom and dad are talkin' to the preacher."

"Oh. That's nice."

"No. It's not nice. My brother keeps runnin' away and he's smokin' cigarettes and thievin' and hangin' with a bad bunch. Sheriff Bodine hauled him into jail when Brody got caught joyriding in Eddie Housen's snowplow. Eddie wasn't too happy since he just got a new scoop for the front of his pickup. He's real picky about that old truck, don't know why since it looks like a big ugly army tank. Mama was cryin', though, and Papa was yellin' and Brody cursed right to their face. Mama said she's at her wits' end, and they're in there talking to Pastor Dan for answers."

Well. She hadn't asked for the whole family history, but she'd gotten it anyway. The little boy was obviously scared, looking toward the door several times. His world was on shaky ground. His parents couldn't control their son and didn't have the answers. Frightening thing for a child when your parents didn't have answers.

Amy could relate. More times than not, she'd had to be the adult in her household, providing the answers when her mother would wring her hands over one dilemma or the other.

She went over to the end table and picked up her camera. "Can I take your picture?"

"Why?"

"Because you're cute."

He grinned. "Okay. My school pictures sucked."

Hmm. Must have picked that word up from the brother. "I'll make you a new one."

"How are you gonna get it to me?"

"I have my own room where I develop the pictures. I can get a copy to Pastor Dan and he can give it to you."

"Okay." He set aside the little metal car he'd been running back and forth over the rug and stood, posing by the fireplace, one hand resting against the bricks, his ankles crossed.

Amy grinned. It was a pose that deserved a man's silk smoking jacket. Except that the subject through her viewfinder was hardly a man, just a little boy with dirt under his fingernails and tennis shoes with the laces untied and dragging on the ground.

"Can I take your picture now?" he asked when she'd taken several shots.

She usually didn't let children mess with her camera. But this little boy needed a distraction.

"Sure." She showed him how to look through the viewfinder and press the shutter, then sat down on the couch and gave him a bright smile.

He made a grand effort to keep the camera still, to stare through the viewfinder until he was certain of his focus, then took the picture, lowering the camera and giving her such a sweet smile, her heart twisted.

She patted the sofa cushions beside her. "Come sit and tell me about school."

Instead of sitting next to her, he climbed into her lap. At first she froze, unsure what to do. He smelled of little boy sweat and peanut butter. Then she wrapped her arms around his skinny body and hugged him to her.

For a woman who'd had very little contact with

children before, she was getting more than her quota now.

Amazingly, it felt more right than she would have imagined.

WHEN DAN CAME OUT of the office with the Cransons, the sight that greeted him made him pause. With the lights low in the living room, Amy sat on the couch, her dark head bent over the redheaded freckle-faced boy.

One of the problems about these counseling sessions was that children shouldn't be present to hear details and so were left out, where they would usually build even greater fears because they knew something was wrong.

Once again, he was struck by Amy's behavior.

The behavior of a minister's wife.

She was beautiful, and caring, unable to resist a person in need. A lot like himself.

She wasn't what he was looking for in a woman...she was so much more. And that scared him.

He saw the Cransons to the door, then went back into the living room. His emotions were all over the place.

He stoked the fire in the hearth, then sat down beside her. Wind pelted the windows, making him glad the Cransons had come to the rectory rather than him having to go out to their place.

"Everything all right?" Amy asked.

He sighed. "That's one troubled family."

"I know. Jeremy spilled the whole story. I didn't ask, mind you. He volunteered."

Dan smiled. He knew she wouldn't have probed. She was a private woman, respected other people's boundaries. "Thanks for keeping him company."

"I didn't mind. He's a sweet boy."

"Amazing how two children in the same family can be so different. That's one of the Cransons' worries. That Jeremy will glamorize his brother's behavior and follow his footsteps."

"I don't think so. He's pretty scared over the whole thing. Were you able to help them?"

"I don't know. I hope so. Sometimes it just helps to talk, to know that there's someone else in your corner who cares. I'll talk to Lester Russo. This is Brody's first arrest and Eddie's not pressing charges over the kids taking his truck. Besides, it was another boy who did the driving. I'll ask Lester to turn Brody over to me, have him serve some community service hours here at the church. Who knows. Maybe I'll be able to get through to him."

She reached over and slipped her hand beneath his, entwining their fingers, then gave a squeeze. "If anybody can, it'll be you."

The support touched him. How many times had he agonized after one of these counseling sessions, alone, no one to share his concerns with?

He raised their linked hands, pressed his lips to her knuckles. Her eyes widened and her breath was suspended.

She was an amazing woman. She'd come into his

life so unexpectedly. What had begun as helping out a woman in need had grown into something more.

So much more.

When he wasn't looking, she'd sneaked beneath his skin and right into his heart.

He pulled her to him, lifted her onto his lap and followed through on the instincts that were screaming inside him, instincts he had no way of stopping, didn't want to stop. He kissed her.

If she had fought him, hesitated, he might have come to his senses. But she returned his kiss, turned his mind to mush and his body to a pulsing, raging mass of need.

Slipping his arm beneath her knees, he stood and carried her toward the stairs.

Amy came out of her sensual stupor for an instant. "Dan?"

He continued up the stairs and into the master bedroom.

"Are you sure about this?" she asked.

For an answer, he lowered his head again and kissed her slowly, thoroughly, blanking her mind of everything but the sensual feel of his clever lips against hers.

He stood her beside the bed, clicked on the lamp. Buttery light cast soft shadows over the room as the wind howled beyond the inky blackness of the windowpanes.

Her heart pounded in anticipation, yet he took his time, watching her, drinking her in.

With his hands tenderly cupping her face, he lowered his head and kissed her again. She thought about the photograph, the wedding kiss, the kiss she'd seen her grandfather give her grandmother. This was the same, yet different. If felt special. It felt like love, but could it be?

She could stand here and kiss him for hours. He was an expert, taking her mouth slowly, not rushing, not blazing ahead and demanding entrance. He gave her time to get used to the feel of his lips on hers, the smell of his skin, the texture of his mouth. Then slowly, ever so slowly, he ran his tongue over the seam of her lips, asking for more.

She didn't think twice about giving the permission he sought. She was so turned on, she wanted to rush, to climb up his body, to eat at his lips.

She whimpered, surprising herself.

"Easy. We have all the time in the world."

No, they didn't. She knew it and he knew it. But for now, they could shut out the world. Shut out the wind against the window, the responsibility of the child sleeping down the hall, the attorney who had a deadline circled on his calendar to satisfy the terms of a will.

His hands slid down her arms, his fingers entwining with hers. Lifting their joined hands, he kissed her knuckles as he'd done downstairs, his gaze locking onto hers.

A lump formed in her throat. There was no excuse for it, no understanding. Just that simple gesture, and her world went off kilter.

Glancing down, feeling the need to hide from the emotions, her gaze landed on the wall socket. He had a hula-dancer night-light.

Okay, everybody needed a light so they wouldn't stub their toe on the way to the bathroom, but a hula dancer?

Somehow, that silly night-light—a symbol of something that was so typically male, so typically normal—made this all seem okay.

Reverently, as though unwrapping a coveted package, he eased the open shirt from her shoulders, untucked the hem of her T-shirt and pulled it over her head.

Her bra was sage-green satin, designed to give extra lift. She might wear men's clothes on the outside, but beneath, her indulgence was for satin and lace and sex appeal.

"I had an idea you'd wear something like this." With a single finger, he stroked the mounds of flesh plumped up by small push-up pads in her bra. "Ever since you described your working lingerie, I've not had a good night's sleep."

She licked her lips. "Um, I've had a few sleepless nights after our run-in with you in the towel."

He grinned. "Good. I like to know you've been thinking about me."

It was difficult to think about anything else. He was such a masculine man, had such presence. Whenever he walked into a room, he commanded attention.

He unhooked the front fastening of her bra, taking his time, let the cups hang open, traced the outer swell of her breasts, coming close but never touching the center. She thought she'd go mad.

He slipped the straps off her shoulders, and she reached for his shirt, tugging it over his head.

"To even the score," she said.

"Let's not get too even. I want this to last."

His chest was wide and firm and muscular. He was the epitome of masculinity. One would never associate him with the clergy. At least not one with preconceived notions of what such men should look like. Amy was fast learning not to judge a book by its cover.

He eased her down on the bed and removed her pants and panties, then took an inordinate amount of time slipping off her socks, massaging her feet, running his lips over the skin he exposed.

Chills raced over her body.

When he stood to remove his own clothes, her tongue stuck to the roof of her mouth. She'd seen him nearly naked, and her imagination had taken it from there. Reality was so much better than imagination.

Her gaze traveled over his flat stomach, farther down.

Oh…my…gosh.

Fully aroused, he was gorgeous.

He eased onto the bed, brushed her hair back from her temples, stared into her eyes for what seemed an aeon, then kissed her.

Her nipples puckered, from the chill in the air or desire, she wasn't sure which. His chest pressed against the sensitized nubs, rubbing, warming, inflaming.

Part of her realized this was wrong, that they shouldn't be traveling this particular road. But she couldn't have denied either of them if her very life depended on it.

"I've dreamed of you like this," he said. "Soft and warm and responsive."

She sucked in a breath as his lips cruised over her neck, her collarbone, her breast, at last closing over her nipple.

Like a string tugging straight from the core of her, her insides tightened, stunning her, shooting her straight into a climax. That had never happened before, and oddly enough, she felt a twinge of both wonder and embarrassment.

He didn't give her time to linger on the phenomenon, for his hands were moving now, stroking between her legs, his fingers slipping inside, first one, then two. Her hips bucked.

A part of her brain realized he was doing all the giving and she was doing the taking, but she couldn't seem to find the wherewithal to participate. Her limbs felt paralyzed with pleasure.

When the second orgasm slammed through her, she screamed, stunned, because she'd had no idea she was a screamer.

This was a first.

He grinned down at her. "Very responsive."

She would have attempted to turn the tables on him, to show him she knew a trick or two to make him respond as well, but his lips were busy again, cruising over her body, lingering here, toying there.

His hands gripped her thighs, lifting her legs, and then he was kissing her in the most intimate way a man could kiss a woman. Again there was a fleeting shiver of perplexity. She was out of control, and that frightened her. She wanted to object, to tell him it was too much.

She was on fire, burning from the inside out. She didn't have breath enough to speak, could only feel, respond.

She gripped the sheets, screamed his name, had a moment of lucidity wondering if she'd wake the baby.

Then he was moving up her body, entering her, turning her mind to mush.

She was brought down to earth with a jolt when he jerked out of her, hissed a word that sounded suspiciously like a curse. Confused, she watched him fumble with the drawer at the bedside, heard something bounce against the floor.

Oh, she thought, when she saw the foil packet he was ripping open with his teeth. A condom. What in the world was he doing with condoms in his bedside drawer?

She could have told him she was on the pill. It kept her regular—every twenty-eight days without fail. It took the guesswork out of her body's time clock, assured her she'd be prepared, wouldn't have an accident when she was in the middle of an assignment, possibly blowing the opportunity for a perfect photo.

"Sorry about that," he murmured.

As though worried that the interruption had drenched the mood, he stroked her body again. She tried to tell him she was already as aroused as she could get, but he silenced her protests with his lips, showed her how wrong she was.

Her own hands were feverish now, touching him where she could, urging him to give her what she desperately wanted, the feel of him inside her, all of him.

At last, he slid inside her once more, slowly, watching her. In and out. Once, twice. She lost count. It could have been hours or minutes, as time lost all meaning. Then he thrust hard and high, and Amy, barely aware, screamed again.

Her body convulsed and she felt him grow incredibly hard inside her, felt him swell, go rigid, murmur her name as he found his own release.

For endless moments, he stayed where he was, allowing them both to wring every glorious drop of pleasure from the pulsating aftermath of their union. Then he rolled off her and shifted her until she was lying against his side, his arms around her, holding her safe.

With the edge of desire sated, rational thoughts returned.

Oh, my gosh. What had they done? By encouraging him, lusting after him, letting their relationship progress to this explosive conclusion, she'd put him in a terrible position.

He could probably still get an annulment based on the fact that the marriage would only last for three months. She wasn't sure, but she thought those were grounds.

Still, he'd also be in a position of having to lie to a lawyer or judge, telling them they didn't have carnal knowledge of each other when they did. And if he didn't fudge, and she was wrong about the three-month time limit being good enough grounds for an annulment, she'd just sentenced him to the stigma of divorce.

She ought to be strung up by her fingernails. Never mind that it had taken both of them to do what they'd just done in this bed.

She wanted to apologize. Didn't know how. Tears burned at the back of her eyes, and all she could do was wrap her arms around his chest and hold him close.

Chapter Eleven

When the phone rang in the middle of the night, this time, Amy was with him.

She rolled over, realized she was naked and felt a moment of self-consciousness. The tone of Dan's voice banished any remnants of sleep or thoughts of herself.

"How bad is it?" he asked, his voice tight, worried. "Okay. I'm on my way."

He hung up the phone and got out of bed. Holding the sheet to her breast, she reached over and switched on the lamp, not wanting him to stub his toe. The hula dancer put out enough light to see by, but no sense in him straining his eyes when she was already awake.

"What is it?" she asked.

"A fire on the reservation. Three homes are involved so far, and it's spreading. The rec center is in danger of going up next. I'm part of the volunteer fire department. Cheyenne and Chance are already on their way out there. I'll meet up with Stony, Wyatt and the Callahans and be right behind them."

Since his back was turned as he was getting

dressed, she found her shirt and shrugged into it. The tails came down to midthigh, so she was perfectly modest.

"Can I do anything to help?"

He pulled a thermal shirt over his head, tucked it into his jeans, then added a flannel shirt on top of that. "Just hold down the fort here with Shayna. I'll call if I get a chance." Tying a bandanna around his neck, he stepped into his boots and grabbed his coat and gloves and jammed his hat on his head.

"All right. Dan?"

He turned at the doorway.

"Be careful."

"Yeah." He winked. "I've got a little extra protection on my side."

Amy couldn't go back to sleep. Her mind insisted on creating all sorts of horrible scenarios of what might be going on. She'd met the people on the reservation, bonded with them, laughed with them and listened as they lovingly complained about their husbands, bragged on their children, gossiped and told wonderful stories about ancient legends.

As the hours ticked by in slow motion and still Dan hadn't called, she worried over what had burned, who had lost their home, if anyone was hurt. She needed to do something, take action.

By the time the sun rose over the horizon, she'd already drunk a whole pot of coffee. Dressing, she paced, waiting for Shayna to wake up. Wouldn't you know? She spent so much time trying to coax the baby into sleep, and now she was wearing a hole in the hallway carpet, making enough noise to jar pecans off a tree.

Impatience winning out, she went into the nursery. "Shayna," she called softly. "Wake up, baby girl."

The baby turned her head, her eyes blinking open like a tiny owl. "You possum. You were already awake, weren't you?"

Shayna gave such a sweet smile Amy felt her heart clinch. "Up we go, sugar. We have to get you dressed and fed. We've a rescue mission to organize." Holding the child's warm body to her chest for a moment, just to please herself, she kissed Shayna's pudgy cheek, then laid her on the bed to change a soggy diaper and dress her in a little bitty sweats outfit. A blue one.

"I'm not messing with a bow, so you can just deal with the color, okay?"

An hour later, Amy was waiting outside Tillis's General store for Vern or Vera to arrive. Chances were Vern might have gone out to the reservation to fight the fire.

Vera drove up, and Iris Brewer was right behind her.

"Amy. You're up and out early. How's the baby?"

"Fine. You heard about the fire at the reservation, didn't you?"

"Yes, Vern and Lloyd went out to help. They both got home about an hour ago. Some of the men are still there, but the fire is out. One of the homes is a total loss, but they were able to save the other two."

"And the rec center?"

"The fire didn't make it that far, thank the Lord."

"Do they know what happened?"

"A propane explosion."

"Oh, my gosh. Was anyone hurt?"

"That I don't know, dear. Vern didn't say."

Amy nodded. "Listen. I'm pretty sure Dan's still out there. I'd like to go check on things for myself, take out some supplies. If people have lost their homes, they'll need food and blankets and toiletries. And...I need a sitter for Shayna."

"Of course, dear. Iris and I will be happy to mind her for you."

"Thank you. I've got a diaper bag packed, but I also left the house open. If you need anything, or want to sit with her over there, just go on in."

"We'll be fine. Now let's gather up the supplies so you can get out to the reservation."

"Let me just get my checkbook out of the diaper bag."

"Don't be silly. This is on us. Neighbors always help neighbors."

"Well, since I'm a neighbor, also, I'd like to contribute."

Vera patted Amy's hand. "We're very lucky to have you with us, dear."

SHE SAW DAN'S TRUCK at the reservation, but no sight of him.

She was dismayed to see that the fire had leveled the very home she'd been to the other day when she'd joined the weaving circle. The charred remnants of the loom rested in the rubble of ashes and water. Amazingly enough, a lone spool of orange yarn spared by the licks of flame rested among the destruction like a misshapen Halloween pumpkin grinning over the trick.

More than the home, the loss of that loom bothered her. It was a purely selfish thought that shamed her.

Opening the back door of her Jeep, she hoisted out a box of supplies, jolting when a man appeared beside her, unsmiling and serious. He was tall, moved silently, with gray hair tied back with a leather band. The way he carried himself, she had an idea he was some sort of leader in this community.

"I am John White Cloud," he said, his voice quiet. "You would be the holy man's wife."

It momentarily took her aback to be identified as such. "Amy," she corrected, needing to retain her own identity. "I wasn't sure what was needed, but I brought some supplies."

He nodded and relieved her of the box she held. "They will be appreciated."

Since her hands were free, she reached back in the Jeep for the second carton, then followed him into a modest home where Jenny White Cloud was already sorting through her own belongings, clothes and linens separated into piles, evidently to offer to whoever was rendered homeless by the fire.

"Amy. It is good of you to come." Jenny abandoned her task to envelop Amy in a warm hug. "It is sad that your visit has caught us in a position of impaired hospitality."

"Don't be silly. I didn't come to be entertained. I brought some things I hope you can use. Tell me what happened. Is everyone all right?"

"Yes, thank *Ma'heo'o*. The child of my sister put flame to a lantern and left it sitting by the propane tank."

"Was she injured?"

"No. John, my husband, sensed something would happen. He has a gift, you see. He was out walking the streets, as was my cousin, Joe Little Coyote. It was Joe who went into the flames to rescue the family. We were very lucky."

"What can I do to help?"

"Your gifts are plenty. The men will clear the mess, begin to rebuild."

"Then I won't keep you or get in your way. Please convey my condolences to your sister's family."

It would take more than mere supplies to set things right, Amy realized as she let herself out of the house. Her eyes strayed once more to that weaving loom on the ruined porch.

She sat on the steps, took out her checkbook and wrote a check, leaving the payee blank. John White Cloud sat down beside her, startling her. How did such a big man move so silently?

"That is not necessary. We will rebuild the loom."

How had he known what was on her mind? His steady, knowing eyes gave her an eerie feeling.

"Then use the money for the materials, or however you see fit."

He nodded, folded the check and put it in his pocket. "You have a generous and giving heart. You were chosen, I believe. And *Ma'heo'o* has chosen well. You are on a journey of discovery. Answers will not come in faraway places, but inside yourself. You will remember that I told you this.''

Leaving her dazed and confused, he stood and walked away. Cryin' all night. Had she just had her fortune told?

Shaking her head, she stood and walked back to her Jeep, pausing as the lure of destruction called to her. Like a passing motorist at a freeway crash, she couldn't help but stare.

The acrid smell of smoke and charred wood permeated the brisk winter air. The high winds they'd had last night must have whipped the fire into a frenzy, causing it to sweep by the neighbors' homes, as well.

A child's stuffed toy lay in the rubble, blackened across the belly as though a renegade flame had merely needed a single lick to quench its craving.

Too bad the craving hadn't stopped there. Destruction created images of helplessness.

She'd sat on that porch mere weeks ago, learning to weave. There had been laughter and silliness and women-talk. Now there was sorrow. The family who'd lived here would be taken in by neighbors, but cherished, irreplaceable heirlooms would be forever lost.

She retrieved her camera, noticed an old man squatting by the brick fireplace left standing, picking through the ravaged debris, his bandaged hands covered in soot.

Joe Little Coyote. The medicine man who pined for his wife, had lost hope.

She wondered if saving a child's life had restored a portion of that hope.

She raised her camera, took a single picture, then covered the lens and turned. Dan stood right behind her.

"Dan." Giddiness shot a warm glow through her at the sight of him. She'd been worried about him.

"I might have known."

Her smile faded. She'd never heard anger in his tone before, seen it on his face. Disgust. Disappointment.

It was there, vibrating in the air like static from a vicious lightning bolt.

Her defensive shield immediately went up. Dan Lucas had a temper. Well hallelujah, call out the dogs. The man was human.

"Where's Shayna?" he asked.

"Vera and Iris are watching her." She noted that his hands were fisted at his side, his clothes streaked with soot. A muscle ticked in his jaw.

"Did you pawn her off so you could attend to your own needs? Prey on these people's misfortune for your own gain? Come out here and snap pictures like a ghoul? Is this what your life is about, Amy?"

With each terse question, her heart pounded harder, words crowding her throat. She wanted to scream in her own defense.

But pride kept her silent. Just as pride had kept her silent when Gramps had cut her to the quick by making a snap judgment when he'd seen her working at the bar. It still hurt that he'd died being disappointed in her. She'd wanted his approval.

And, she realized, she wanted Dan Lucas's approval. Where the hell was her rebel alter ego when she needed it? The one that snubbed convention, convinced her that what others thought of her didn't matter a hill of beans.

The problem was, it mattered a lot.

Her heart stung as though swarmed by a thousand angry wasps. Salty tears burned at the back of her nose and eyes.

She lifted her chin. Her first instinct was to rip the film out of the camera and throw it in his face. She checked the impulse. She wouldn't give him the satisfaction.

Instead, she merely turned without speaking and walked away.

DAN WATCHED HER DRIVE AWAY, suddenly ashamed of his behavior, surprised at the white-hot anger that had swept him when he'd come around the corner and seen her taking pictures.

He hadn't lashed out at another person like that in a long time. And why had he? Because she'd left Shayna with a sitter? There was nothing wrong with that.

It was the reminder that photography would take her away. She would leave, in search of opportunities just like this.

John White Cloud walked across the street, stood silently for a moment, staring at the charred homes that Dan's unseeing eye was trained on.

"We will rebuild," he said quietly. "The donations

are appreciated. I will send a letter of gratitude that you will read to your church.''

''Yes,'' he said automatically. Then his fuzzy brain focused on the words. What donation?

''You will convey once again my thanks to your wife.'' John pulled a check from his shirt pocket.

Dan frowned.

''It is for a new weaving loom,'' John said. ''I told your wife we could build a replacement, that the gift of money was too large. She has pride and a good heart. A pride I recognize and did not want to bruise. So, I accept your gift, with many thanks.''

Dan looked at the check. That was a huge chunk of her savings, he was sure. Her travel fund.

He felt like a jerk for jumping to conclusions.

He imagined that was exactly what John White Cloud was attempting to show him.

''The gift is from Amy. I had nothing to do with it.''

''I know.''

Dan sighed. ''I'm a fool.''

''As we all are at times. Even holy men make mistakes.'' Refolding the check and returning it to his pocket, he walked away, leaving Dan standing in the middle of the street.

The last time he'd stood nearly in this same spot, watching Amy take pictures, play with the children, interact with the local women, he'd been thinking she was acting just like a minister's wife would.

Today, she really had been. In the true spirit of giving, without expecting recognition or praise.

AMY HAD PLENTY OF TIME to lick her wounds, to replay the conversation in her mind, to realize that Dan was tired, to see things from his angle.

She sat in the rocking chair, cuddling Shayna, even though the child slept. Dan's anger made her feel vulnerable. Holding on to Shayna seemed to lessen the breathlessness. She couldn't say why.

Did she equate anger with loss?

Gramps had been angry and she'd lost him. Would she lose this baby, and Dan, too?

Her thoughts were unreasonable. Of course she would lose both. Not to death. But by her own leaving. This wasn't for keeps. Why did she keep forgetting that lately?

Her heart lurched when she heard the front door open, then saw Dan a moment later. He paused by the door to the living room, as though unsure of his welcome.

For pity's sake. It was his home.

"I'm sorry," he said.

She wasn't prepared for the immediate apology. When she and Doyle had fought, he'd turned it around on her, would have eaten a live worm before he'd utter those two words.

"When I saw you taking pictures, I was reminded that photography is your life. That you'll be going back to it."

"I've never hidden that from you. I was up-front about that from the beginning. So why would you think I'd suddenly changed into an insensitive clod?"

"I said I was sorry. I should have known better. I

do know better. I counsel a lot of troubled people. It spills over sometimes.''

Her heart went out to him. Everyone had a breaking point. Dan was perilously close to his.

He saw so much sadness and strife in his business. More than most. Death and sickness and tragedy touched him daily, where the rest of the world went blissfully about their lives, leaving people like Dan to pick up the pieces. Where most people read in the papers about other's troubles, Dan was in the center of it, called out to do what he could to ease.

Little wonder it would touch a nerve when it appeared she'd been capitalizing on another's misfortune.

''Thank you for what you did today.''

She shrugged. ''It was nothing.''

''It was much more than nothing. You saved me a turn-around trip, provided for needs much faster.''

She hadn't done it for thanks and his made her uncomfortable. ''You look tired. Why don't you go shower, get some rest. I'll answer the phones and wake you if it's important.''

He stared at her for a long moment, then nodded and went upstairs. Amy sat where she was for a while longer, gazing down at the sleeping child in her arms.

Finally she got up and took the baby upstairs, putting her in the portable crib, covering her with a fluffy blanket. They should buy a regular crib, she thought.

Then again, what if Cheyenne found someone in Lyssa's extended family who would come here to claim the child? The thought gave her a pang.

Checking the baby monitor and taking the receiver

with her, she left the door partially ajar, feeling a bit adrift, not sure what to do with her time.

As she passed Dan's door, she glanced in. He was sitting on the side of the bed, wearing only a pair of white briefs. His hair was damp from his shower. His elbows were on his knees, his head in his hands.

She hesitated. Was he praying? He looked exhausted. Alone. Sad. As though the burdens he shouldered were finally getting to him.

Making a decision, she went into the room, climbed on the bed behind him and massaged his shoulders. He stiffened, lifted his head.

"Relax," she said. "Let me take care of you for once." He wasn't dressed, but she'd seen him in less.

The muscles beneath her hands were tight. In silence, she manipulated them, soothing. The house was absolutely quiet, broken only by the sound of a jet flying overhead, no doubt carrying excited travelers to places unknown, giddy with anticipation of new worlds to explore.

He reached up and put his hand over hers, stopping her. Gently gripping her wrist, he pulled her around to his lap.

She looked into his chocolate eyes, unable to read his expression.

"I need you."

This, she understood. They'd been dancing around this attraction, the chemistry, since that fiery kiss at the altar. Their lovemaking last night had merely fanned the flame.

She stood and slowly undressed as he watched. When he reached for her, she stayed his hands.

"My turn," she said softly. Urging him back on the bed, she removed his briefs then fitted her body over him.

His palms stroked her back, cupped her behind, pressed her against his arousal.

She could have stayed this way for hours. She rubbed against him, reveling in the fit of their bodies, the size of him. He was a big man, tall and strong and muscular. He made her feel tiny, when she wasn't.

Because he was always the one who gave, she was determined to call the shots. Tenderly, trying to convey just that, she kissed him, tasted his desire, the difficulty he was having giving up control.

As he'd done for her the night before, she moved down his body, mapped it with her hands first, then her lips.

"Amy..."

"Shh. Let me." She spent a long time just kissing him, from his head to his feet, skimming over the parts of him she knew ached for fulfillment.

The need to give was total. She stroked him, took him in her mouth.

"Oh, man..."

Heady with her own power, she gave, deriving more pleasure than she could have imagined in the giving. She knew she was testing his limits, and that, too, thrilled her—that this strong man trusted her enough to give himself over to her.

She knew she'd pushed as far as he'd allow when his hands fisted in her hair. "I need..."

"I know what you need." She slid up his chest,

straddled him and lowered her body, taking him inside by exquisitely slow inches.

His hands gripped her hips, held her still. "Give me a minute."

She wasn't sure if she could. The feel of him pulsing inside her built, an urgency that wouldn't be denied.

She gazed down at him, saw him watching her. The look on his face was all-encompassing. She'd never been the absolute object of a man's attention this way. It was a novel experience.

She moved against him, taking her time, eyes locked as tightly as their bodies. His hands molded her breasts, and when he raised up and closed his mouth over her nipple, she bit her lip to hold back a scream.

It was that momentary lapse that allowed him to take control. In one smooth move, he shifted their positions, pulled her beneath him, and made love to her with an urgency that was nearly frightening.

Desire and terrifyingly swift emotions flooded her too fast to identify, making it impossible to hold on to a single one for more than seconds at a time before another surged.

She couldn't breathe, couldn't think.

Her body throbbed, her muscles contracting.

The orgasm that whipped through her pushed him over the edge as well. She rode the crest, took his burdens, held him to her with arms that wanted to cling, a heart that wanted to stop the clock.

When they'd both recovered their breath, he gazed

down at her, kissed her with a tenderness that made her want to weep.

"Thank you," he murmured.

That made her smile. "My pleasure, I'm sure. Though you cheated. It was my turn to be in the driver's seat."

"Next time."

He tucked her beside him and it wasn't long before she heard the even sound of his breathing.

There shouldn't be a next time. She shouldn't allow it.

But she knew she would.

If he needed her, for as long as she was here, she would be his anchor.

Shayna slept peacefully down the hall, a monitor on the nightstand turned on so they'd hear her if she woke.

A family, she thought. She'd never dreamed her life would turn out this way.

The problem was, this wasn't her fairy tale. It wasn't what she'd planned for, dreamed of. Oh, someday, sure. But not this soon.

By continuing with the intimacy, was she setting them both up with a false sense of security?

Even if she *could* stay, how would she know if it was for real? How would she know if the relationship was enduring only because it had been consummated? Or because he needed a two-parent family for Shayna's sake?

And when, she asked herself, had she become such a pessimist? Questioned her worth?

When her father had failed to come home night after night, she realized.

When her mother had become needy and dependent.

When the country club crowd had turned so judgmental.

When Gramps had expressed his disappointment.

She'd pined for her father, taken care of her mother, snubbed the country club folks and ached over Gramps's censure.

Despite her behavior to the contrary, she'd agonized over what everyone else thought of her.

And she was doing it again. With Dan.

Chapter Twelve

The first official day of spring brought snow. It was beautiful, a waterfall of white confetti piling on the roof of the barn, the rounded top of the fence rail, mounding on the steps of the church.

Dan watched it from the study window. Odd, how spring signified new buds, change, growth. The snow would stunt that growth for a while yet.

The phone rang in the office and he reached for it.

"Cheyenne here, Dan."

"Cheyenne. How's the family?"

"Emily and the babies are fine. Heck, you probably see my wife as often as I do. I saw the latest mock-up for the church bulletin. If you're not careful, she'll turn it into a ten-page, full-color brochure."

Dan laughed. "Emily's advertising expertise has increased our church budget tenfold. I'm not messing with her methods."

"Mmm-hmm," Cheyenne murmured. "Wait till you see what her next idea is."

Dan laughed again. "Since I don't think you're about to tell me, I'll wait. I love her surprises." Sobering, he asked, "And how are the rest of the family? Your uncle's people?"

"Great. Everyone's settled back in—thanks again for your help."

Jake McCall, the developer in town, had temporarily suspended work on the hotel and taken his crew over, donating his services to rebuild the ruined homes. Dan had joined the rest of the guys in the area, along with the men on the reservation, and they'd completed the project within a week.

"No problem." One of the best things to come out of the near tragedy was the change in Joe Little Coyote. The medicine man was practicing again, had pulled out of his downward spiral that'd had him merely existing, waiting for the Great Spirit he believed in to take him home.

Saving the life of a child had given him back his faith in his power to heal. His worth on this earth.

"I called to report on Lyssa Farly," Cheyenne said.

Dan's heart lurched. "Did you find family members?"

"I traced back through the foster families. That poor girl went through a mess. The parents signed away their legal rights when she was five. I hate to speculate on why—it's probably best that we don't. Anyway, there's no trace of them, and it wouldn't matter if there was. By signing away their right to Lyssa, there are no legal ties to the child. And frankly, that's probably a blessing. So, I guess your next step, now that we've determined that there's no next of kin to take the child, is to contact social services."

"I'm not putting this baby in foster care. I promised Lyssa I'd care for her."

"That's what you want?"

"Yes." More than he'd ever realized until this moment.

"Then you'll want to apply for legal guardianship or adoption, in which case you can go directly through the courts. I can send over papers to fill out beforehand, make some calls and set something up for you."

"Thanks, buddy. I'd appreciate it."

He hung up the phone and stared out at the white snow. Spring would bring change, after all.

Official parenthood.

He was anxious to get on with the adoption proceedings, but how would he explain his and Amy's arrangement when the court investigator came out for the interview?

Should he simply leave things as they were for now and wait three more weeks? She'd likely be gone by then.

He knew the courts would let a single parent adopt. Heck, movie stars were doing it right and left.

He imagined the investigative team would counsel him on the benefits of a two-parent household—as he would have done if he were counseling a potential adoptive parent.

Because he believed a child was better off in a two-parent household. Right now, he was providing that for Shayna. But what about a month from now?

He instinctively put his hand over his wallet resting in his back pocket where Lyssa's letter was folded.

Promise me.

Although the chances were excellent that Shayna wouldn't have any trouble being placed if he chose to give her up, there were no guarantees that the home she might go to would *remain* stable, no way to guarantee she would be loved as he could love her, raised as Lyssa wanted her raised.

Stony Stratton had taken in his goddaughter—who was no blood relation to him. He'd been a single man at the time, hadn't run into any problems with the courts, had been the best father, the perfect father for little Nikki.

Dan had to do the same for Shayna.

He'd made a promise. He couldn't, *wouldn't* break that promise.

Maybe it was wrong to deliberately wait, to shy away from questions that had no easy answers, steer clear of explanations that would certainly raise red flags with a court-appointed investigator.

But everything, their whole lives, were up in the air right now. Intimacy wouldn't hold Amy. God knows, he wished it would.

In the meantime, he didn't want to rock the boat, take a chance on losing both of them. It would be hard enough letting Amy go. If he lost Shayna too…

He still had three weeks. Miracles could happen.

And he was a man who believed in them.

Turning away from the window, he followed the smell of pot roast…and baking. Something sweet and mouthwatering.

He paused outside the kitchen doorway. With Shayna riding on her chest facing forward in the backpack sling, kicking her legs and gurgling, Amy was keeping up a constant stream of conversation with the baby.

"Don't you put your toes in my chocolate cake. Here, now, doodle-bug, we'll have to have a bath before supper." She snatched a dishrag and wiped the baby's feet. "I let you go barefooted because it's nice and toasty in the kitchen. That's no call for you to run amok like a calf in clover. Don't tell, now. I'll just give a swipe with the spreader, here, and nobody'll be the wiser."

"Teaching her to fib, are we?"

Amy jumped and chocolate whipped right off the spatula and down the front of Shayna's sling. A splatter landed on the baby's chin and her little tongue worked its way out, drool dribbling like clear molasses onto the front of the bib.

Dan laughed, retrieved the dishrag she'd discarded only moments ago, and dabbed at Shayna's face and the front of the sling, prompting a giggle as the movements tickled her tummy.

Amy smiled. The sound of a child's laughter was so heartwarming.

Figuring it worked once, he tried it again and was rewarded with another belly laugh. Amy had to sit down. She was getting hysterical just watching Dan's crazy faces, the way he was entertaining the baby.

"Now you've got her wound up and she's not going to want to settle down and let me take her out of this sling."

"Were you planning to take her out?"

"Yes. I have to get the roast out of the oven. Those

little feet of hers are busier than a sack full of tomcats. Smearing her toes in the cake's one thing. Hot gravy's out of the question.''

''I'll take her. She's nearly sitting up on her own, now. We should get her a high chair.''

''That's a good idea. Have you checked the attic to see if there's one up there?''

He frowned. ''No.''

''Didn't you grow up here?''

''Yes.''

''Were you or any of your brothers born here?''

''I was. I'm the youngest.''

''Then there's a good chance treasures are hiding in the attic.''

''I'll check. I haven't been up there in years.''

She grinned at him. ''Scared of the spiders?''

''Maybe. Want to go up with me and protect me?''

''As a matter of fact, I love to explore. You go give the baby a bath since you got her dirty and I'll finish up dinner.''

''I didn't get her dirty,'' he objected. ''You're the one who slung chocolate from here to kingdom come.''

''Oh, that's a bit of an overstatement, wouldn't you say? And I wouldn't have slung it if you hadn't scared me half to death.''

''It was your guilty conscience. Encouraging our daughter to fib.''

The minute the words were out, they both fell silent.

Our daughter.

He cleared his throat. ''Cheyenne called.''

"And?"

"Lyssa's birth parents signed away their rights to her when she was a little girl."

"A little girl? Not a baby?"

"Evidently they kept her for a while. Cheyenne didn't want to go into the particulars, and I'm just as glad he didn't. The point is, they're nowhere to be found, and it wouldn't matter if they were. They have no rights."

"That's horrible. And the poor thing never got adopted into a stable family."

"No."

The life Lyssa went through didn't bear thinking about. "So, what's next?"

"Cheyenne's going to get me papers for legal guardianship and adoption, set up an appointment so I can talk to an attorney or a judge, I'm not sure which."

Amy gazed at the baby, who was happily trying to get hold of Dan's nose, poking her fingers in his mouth, craning her neck to get his attention.

He looked down at her, held her wandering fingers away from his mouth and kissed her cheek, which got her legs pumping and her free arm waving.

She was getting so cute, developing such a personality. At five months, she was ready to crawl, had two bottom teeth barely showing, and she'd begun to light up when Amy came into the room.

Before, she'd responded better to Dan.

Now, she had a tendency to cling to Amy.

Oh, my gosh. This was exactly what she hadn't planned on. To let her heart get involved.

With the child or with the man.

But she had. And it was wrong, wrong, wrong.

Because she *had* to go. The plans were set. She'd promised herself. Promised her father.

She figured Dan had simply slipped when he'd said *our* daughter. Raising Shayna was his vow to Lyssa.

And hadn't he just said Cheyenne was making a court date for *him?* Not *us.*

She shouldn't worry. Shayna would be fine with Dan. He was a good father. He would raise her well. It wasn't her responsibility to worry.

Her role in all this was simply to help out while she was here.

"You better go get her bathed or this roast will be tough as a sow's snout."

AFTER DINNER, when Shayna was asleep in bed, Dan pulled down the folding attic stairs and they climbed up to the loft.

It was spacious enough to stand up, could have been a third story on the house. Not that it was needed. The house was huge as it was.

A thick layer of dust covered every surface, stirring as they walked across the creaky plank floor.

"You were right," he said, nodding toward the corner. "There's the high chair."

Cobwebs clung to the wood tray, covered the fabric safety belt like an army of mealybugs. A soapy wash-cloth would set things to right.

"Contrary to my brave words, spiders give me the willies, so you're on your own moving this thing."

He grinned and winked. "I'll protect you."

"My hero." Picking her way across the squeaking floor, she ran her hand over an old cedar chest and wiped her dusty hand on the seat of her jeans.

"Seems a shame to keep a piece of furniture this beautiful tucked away up here."

"Do you have any idea how heavy that thing is? I'm *not* muscling it down those stairs. It can just stay up here and beautify the attic."

He came up beside her, bent down to lift the lid on the chest.

"Hey, look at all this stuff. I wondered where these old trophies went."

"Football?"

"Yeah." He lifted a tarnished award. "Most valuable player. Pretty cool, huh?"

Typical guy. "What position did you play?"

"Defensive line."

Mmm. Which explained the linebacker shoulders. She picked up a photo album, opened the leather cover. "Now, this is a shame to hide away. Even I've got enough muscles to get this downstairs."

He took the album from her, sat down and patted the floor next to him. "Pull up a board and have a seat."

She checked for crawly insects, then sat crossedlegged beside him, bending over his shoulder as he turned the pages depicting his family history.

There were tons of family pictures, from boyhood to adulthood. He looked more like his mother, a beautiful woman with a smile that lit her face as though she laughed often and well. Just like Dan.

Phil Lucas and the other two sons, David and Phillip Jr. looked like their father, tall and slim, more reserved.

"After living here so long, why did your dad leave?"

"He was offered a bigger ministry in Wyoming. By that time, I'd completed Bible college, and took over the church here."

"Your brothers weren't interested?"

"David was already established in Missoula. Phillip opted to go with Dad as assistant pastor. I think they knew that this was my dream."

"Must be confusing for your dad's congregation with two Pastor Lucases."

"Phillip never shortened his name—though I call him Pip. He beat the heck out of me a couple of times, especially when I shouted it across the field when he was putting the moves on Sally Roscoe, but when that didn't curb my ornery streak, he gave up."

"You fought?"

"Sure. That's what brothers do."

She wouldn't know, being an only child. She envied his memories, his complete family.

"So, what happened to Sally Roscoe?"

"He married her. Ah, now we come to my rowdy days. Recognize these guys?"

Wyatt Malone, Ethan, Grant and Clay Callahan, Stony Stratton, Chance Hammond and Dan.

"We were quite a group."

"Who's this?" she asked, pointing to a geeky boy who hadn't quite grown into his protruding Adam's apple.

"Eddie Housen."

The guy with the snowplow who didn't have sense enough to take the keys out of the ignition, making it too much of a temptation for teenage boys to resist.

The next picture showed the eight guys wearing ill-fitting suits and looking like they were facing the barrel of a rifle rather than the lens of a camera.

Dan laughed over it. "My mother took this picture, since she rarely saw us all dressed up at the same time. She had no idea we were so hungover we could barely stand the lingering smell of bacon in the air— or maybe she *did* know and that's why she'd had every one of us sitting down to eat a big meal before the funeral."

"You were hungover at a funeral?"

"Yes. My Great-Uncle Earl's. Me and the guys had gone out to the cemetery the night before. Uncle Earl was a cool guy, and he loved his Wild Turkey, so we decided he'd appreciate us drinking a toast to him. The grave was already dug for the funeral scheduled the next day. We got ourselves two twelve-packs of beer and took turns making toasts—there were a lot of memories to drink to."

He laughed again. "I swear somebody must have pushed me—my recollection at that time was a little fuzzy. The guys claim I tipped back my beer bottle, and the next thing they knew I'd toppled face first into the grave."

She sucked in a breath, choked on a laugh. "You didn't."

"Big as you please."

"What did they do?"

"Just stared in like a bunch of drunk idiots. Said, 'Hey, dude, you okay in there?'"

She laughed at his mimic of his friends. "How'd you get out?"

"It wasn't easy. We got to laughing so hard the groundskeeper came shining his flashlight. Since we were disrespecting the dead and my father would be praying over Uncle Earl's soul the next day, the guys hauled my butt out of that hole and made a huddle around me as we slunk off. They figured I had the most to lose if the groundskeeper recognized me and told my dad. We must have looked like a football team doing a running sidestep huddle."

"You *were* a bad boy."

"Everybody's got a past." He closed the album. "What about you? What kind of teenager were you? Cheerleader? Prom queen?"

"No. Photography club. I did actually have a debutante ball at the country club when I was seventeen. Grandpa and Mom insisted. They were big on keeping up appearances."

"And you just wanted to be left alone with your cameras and dreams of faraway worlds."

"Mmm-hum."

"Next came college?"

"Georgia State. Then a job at the town newspaper."

"If you were already employed, how did the cocktail waitress job come about?"

"The newspaper didn't pay squat. My tips at the bar were obscenely huge." Perhaps she shouldn't have used the word *obscene,* given the type of place she'd worked in. She glanced at him to see if he'd judge.

His expression was open and interested.

"Your traveling fund," he said with a nod. "Your grandfather held the deed on the house. Did he pay the expenses as well?"

"Yes. My mom was…dependent, pampered, I suppose. She had a lot of trouble making even the simplest decision on her own. I watched out for her when Dad was traveling. When Dad died, Gramps came to the rescue, determined to take care of both of us. He liked being in control. Then again, so did I, and I'd been doing it for so many years I chaffed a bit against the interference. Which was why we probably butted heads. He wanted to hold the purse strings until I came to my senses and settled down with a nice man and took my place in society like he believed I should."

Dan watched her clasp her hands in her lap. Beneath the oversize casual clothes was a gloss that came from education and wealth.

Which made the situation they were in seem unreal.

Her entire inheritance, her mother's home, rested on their three-month sojourn in marriage, ninety short days that would come to an end in less that three weeks.

She was basically an heiress, and Dan now held the key to her fortune.

Why would a man who'd obviously loved her not support her dreams? See her talent?

"Did you ever show your grandfather your work?"

"A long time ago. It brought up bad feelings about Dad. So, I kept it low-key."

"I'm sorry for that."

She shrugged. "Not your problem."

"So, it's been up to you to keep things running smooth."

"I guess it has. Though I was a little surprised the last time I talked to my mom. She's gotten a job at the local nursery. Something in her voice tells me she's smitten with the owner."

"Does that bother you?"

"It shouldn't. I think it does."

It seemed they were both people who took more responsibility on their shoulders than the average folk. And they both took those responsibilities seriously.

Loyal to a fault.

Which explained Amy's loyalty to her father. Why she worried about another man taking her father's place. Why she worried about missing an opportunity to make a name for herself, as Amy Marshall, Mark Marshall's daughter.

Her tribute to the man who'd saved Dan's father's life.

Because of that, one part of him was rooting for her.

The other part, the selfish part, was rooting for him and Shayna.

Chapter Thirteen

It was Dan's turn to get up with the baby. As he held the bottle steady in Shayna's mouth, he gazed down at her, his heart squeezing.

Ever since Cheyenne's call, he'd been chomping at the bit to make good on his promise, to put the wheels in motion to give this child his name, to fulfill his obligation.

Although he didn't view it as an obligation.

Like his wife, this little baby had wormed her way into his heart.

He couldn't imagine letting her go, couldn't imagine how he had ever got along without her.

He wanted to watch her grow, get her first tooth, take her first step, hold her hand on her first day of kindergarten, watch her fall in love, walk her down the aisle when she joined her life with a man who—he'd make darn sure—would love her and give her the life she deserved.

He wanted a family.

He'd been dedicated to the church and this town for so long. After his breakup with Glenda, he'd felt it wasn't fair to have a relationship that he couldn't give one hundred percent to, so he'd put it out of his mind, never pursued one.

Now an entire family had been dropped into his life, uninvited—first a wife, then a baby, obligating him to carve out time to dedicate to them.

He'd found that it was working. Better than he'd ever imagined.

A family didn't take time away from who he was or what he did.

The overwhelming feelings he had for Amy and Shayna reminded him that he'd been lonely for a very long time now. He'd just never stopped to recognize it.

More than anything, Amy's presence in his life had pointed that out to him. She was persistent, outgoing, sexy. She made him laugh, and she made him burn.

He glanced up as the object of his thoughts came into the room. She wore a silk robe belted at the waist. Beneath, he knew she was naked. The knowledge made his heart beat like a drum.

"Everything okay?" she asked, her voice soft from sleep.

"Fine. Seems like she should be sleeping through the night by now."

"I asked Emily about that. The twins still wake up, but that could be because there's two of them. One bothers the other and then they're both up."

She came over next to the rocking chair, lowered herself to the floor at his feet, hooked an arm over his knee with an easy familiarity he doubted she even realized.

He wished someone was here to grab her camera, snap a picture of the three of them.

A family. Rocking the baby in the still of the night.

"When I took Shayna in for a checkup with Chance, he said all babies advance at different rates."

With her arm still on his knee, she reached with her other hand to stroke the baby's foot. The feel of her breast pressing against his leg was giving him fits.

"Do you think she still misses Lyssa?"

"Maybe." He concentrated on the child in his arms rather than the sexy woman at his feet. "I think she knows she's safe, though."

Amy smiled. "Then maybe she just misses you and can't go more than a few hours without seeing your face."

"What about your face?" he asked carefully.

She didn't seem to pick up on his tone. "Oh, your face is much more handsome. You don't forget to take off your mascara and scare her silly with dark circles under your eyes."

"Probably because I don't *wear* mascara."

"There is that. Did you want me to spell you? I know you've got an early day tomorrow."

"How do you know that?"

"You forget I made out your schedule."

"Yes, and I can't believe you told Thelma Goodman I'd go sit with her while she has her bunions removed."

She grinned. "She's apprehensive about the surgery."

He snorted. "It's hardly surgery. She's a hypochondriac."

"Shame on you."

He sighed. "Yes, well, why don't *you* go sit with her?"

"Because she asked for you. And I've got the Easter committee to deal with. Emily has grand plans. Somebody needs to be there to rein her in."

"Good luck," he said with a laugh that caused Shayna to let go of the nipple of the bottle and grin, milk dribbling out of the corner of her mouth. "You should have seen what she did for the live nativity at Christmastime. We had a traffic jam from Main Street halfway to Billings."

"Well, then, I hope you have an in with a chicken farmer. She's advertising an Easter-egg hunt on the church lawn the Saturday before Easter. I thought it'd make more sense to hold it after the holiday services, or even before, to encourage more people to come hear you preach. I guess there's some other do planned at the Strattons', a sort of tradition, I'm told. Plus, it was pointed out that you'd likely have to move the services since the church wouldn't hold all the extra people. Which doesn't seem like a real hardship to me. I can picture you, standing at the top of Shotgun Ridge Hill, right where Addie Malone stood, preaching to the masses."

He grinned. "Wouldn't do my reputation any good to hold a gun on the parishioners."

She laughed softly and whacked him on the thigh.

"You don't need a gun, Dan. Your charisma is more potent and persuasive than any weapon."

"Hmm. I like compliments."

"It's that ego."

He laughed softly. "If you want to change traditions, go for it. I'll adapt. You might be onto something with Shotgun Ridge though. Instead of the Sermon on the Mount, we'll have a sunrise sermon on the ridge."

Whatever he said caused a look of distress to come over her face.

Tradition, he realized. He could almost read her mind. She didn't believe she had the right to change town tradition when she was only temporary.

Doggone it. Why the heck hadn't he stopped while he was ahead?

"YOU'RE NOT GOING to believe what kind of a day I've had."

Dan laid down his pen, watched her stroll into the study, glancing at a brochure in her hand. She didn't pause, didn't think to ask if she was interrupting, just launched into speech, talking a mile a minute in that Southern voice that put extra syllables on every word. It's a wonder she could gather this much speed.

"I've read 'Mary Had a Little Lamb' a dozen times, but never thought to see it. That silly goat of Hannah's followed her right over to the Callahans. That's where we were meeting today because Ryan had a cold—he slept upstairs, so Shayna wasn't exposed, or any of the other kids for that matter," she said lest he need assurance.

He didn't. Amy was like a mother hen when it came to Shayna.

"Anyway, I swear to goodness, the Callahans' house is something else! I've never seen so many extravagant, big-boy toys in my life. They've got a media center that's a bookshelf on one side, and with the touch of a button, the whole wall changes around like something out of Batman's cave and there it is. Amplifiers and speakers and all manner of decadent equipment..." She stopped, gave him a sheepish grin.

"I imagine you know that, don't you?"

Excitement glowed on that remarkable face. She simply mesmerized him.

She'd adapted to this town, these people—his world—so easily. Pride and love swelled in him, bittersweet emotions that made his heart sing yet pound in dread.

He could lose her. Lose the bright light she shone over his life, a light that bathed him in yearning.

As he gazed into her animated face, everything he wanted, everything he'd never known he dreamed of, melted together in that one moment, that one woman.

She was standing by his side, her thigh nearly brushing his. He pushed his chair back, stood up.

There was one area where they were one hundred percent compatible. And he wasn't above using it to hold the clawing beast inside him at bay, the raw, fearful emotions he tried to ignore when he thought about her leaving, taking away the light.

His hands weren't as gentle as he'd have liked when he maneuvered her in front of him.

He had a moment of satisfaction at her hum of surprise, her sigh of surrender.

And then his hands were on her face, in her hair, his mouth on hers as need fed on need.

She made him crave her to a point that nothing else mattered.

He meant to take it slow, to savor, but the minute her lips opened under his, greed engulfed him. He hoisted her up on the desk, planted his palms on either side of her, trapping her, uncaring of the papers scattered there.

She gave a muffled cry, both thrill and shock.

He wasn't sure where his aggression came from. It was that mobile mouth beneath his, he decided, her utter, liquid surrender. It made a man feel like a king.

It made him want to rule, to control, to see how far he could push before she pushed back.

Because when Amy pushed back, when she threw herself into the moment, it was like nothing he'd ever experienced…and *everything* he'd ever experienced all rolled into one.

"Did you lock the front door?"

"I don't know. I don't remember."

His lips cruised over her neck, drawing a moan. "The baby?"

"Sleeping."

"Don't move."

He closed and locked the study door, then strode back to the desk, tearing at his clothes as he went.

Amy slid off the desk and got a head start on her own clothes, her hands tangling with Dan's as he reached out to help her. Desperate to feel his body against hers, she eased against him, stunned once more when he hauled her back up on the desk.

"Have a care for the papers."

"Right now, I have a *huge* care for you. Only you."

Oh, he always said the right things. Made her feel treasured. Desired.

His hands jerked at her hips, positioning her at the edge of the desk.

A raw cry of delight rose from her throat. "Hurry," she said, certain she'd die if she had to wait another moment. He was like a drug in her system, making her crave more. And more.

She arched her hips and he drove into her in a powerful thrust. She gasped, her gaze locking onto his for endless moments.

"More," she said. And he gave her more, blood heating, flesh straining against flesh, breath ragged as she clawed to hold on, to ride the peak, losing the battle as he shifted, higher, harder.

She cried out, the sound swallowed up as his mouth slammed against hers.

She heard his moan, felt the violent tremors that shook his body as he, too, found release.

Oh, dear heaven, what had this man done to her? She was completely, blindly, joyfully in love with him. A huge, huge problem, but there it was none-theless.

Her hands slid limply to his shoulders.

"Cryin' all night," was all she could manage to say.

He laughed, his body stirring anew inside her.

Her eyes widened. "Again?"

"And again." This time, he carried her over to the

sofa, laid her down and started all over again on a journey toward bliss.

He'd never be able to prepare another sermon on that desk without thinking about Amy atop it, her skin flushed in ecstasy.

For that matter, the memories would probably intrude on his *delivery* of said sermons.

He was going to take a lot of teasing from his friends, he realized. Because they'd surely notice when he lost his place and got all flustered.

The experience was well worth a little teasing and frustration.

THE PROBLEM WITH sticking one's head in the sand was that sooner or later, the laws of nature dictated that one had to come up for air.

Dan took in a lungful and felt it whoosh out again.

With the mail in his hands, shaking, he noted, his gut twisted as he stared at the third envelope.

It was addressed to Amy Marshall, from a travel agent, with the *National Geographic* stamp in the corner.

Airline tickets?

Easter Sunday marked their three-month time limit. It was too late for her to drive back to Georgia. Would she fly directly to Africa from Montana? Would she leave her belongings here for the two months she'd be gone? Make him look at them day in and day out?

Make him yearn?

And would she return after the assignment? Return because she felt trapped? Obligated because of their intimacy?

He had so many questions, and no easy answers.

Dan realized his biggest mistake. Oh, he told himself his intentions were honorable, that he was operating out of love.

But that genuine love could well have trapped Amy. Like a woman deliberately flushing her birth control pills to push marriage, had he made love to her to hold her?

He counseled couples all the time. Why couldn't he figure out his own life?

The one thing he was sure of, though, was that Amy Marshall-Lucas was a beautiful bird who should fly free.

She was excellent at her work. The images and emotions she captured on film simply took his breath away. Her talent was boundless. To hold her back wouldn't be fair.

Oh, she might adjust to life here for a while, but her kind of talent deserved to be set free. It's what she'd wanted her entire life and he had no right to persuade her otherwise.

He'd agreed to the terms of the marriage with no strings.

But that was before he'd fallen in love with her. His wife.

And before they'd been entrusted with a tiny baby. A baby that had brought them together like a true family.

He wanted permanence...and he knew he could never ask for it.

She should have her heart's desire, see the world

she so yearned to see, win that Pulitzer Prize she wanted so much.

He wanted that for her, too.

The problem was, he wanted to be the man standing by her side when she won it.

AMY WORKED LIKE A DEMON, keeping herself so busy there was no time to think.

She'd promised Jenny White Cloud she'd be out to join the weaving circle, be the first to thread a piece of yarn on the new loom.

Ella Sheffield had another chemotherapy treatment scheduled for Wednesday. Amy had gotten in the habit of sitting with Ella, holding her hand when the horrible nausea ravaged her body.

She had five hundred Easter eggs to color, baskets to prepare.

Yet there was an airline ticket waiting for her on the dresser. Dan had brought it in with the mail.

National Geographic hadn't been willing to extend the deadline more than a couple of days. She'd checked. So, they'd mailed the travel arrangements and itinerary here.

And since then, she and Dan had nearly reverted back to being roommates, uncomfortable silences stretching between them, walking on eggshells.

Oh, she still slept in his bed, but he didn't reach for her. She'd lie awake, heart pounding, confused, and he'd just slip his hand beneath hers, hold it tenderly, then finally slide into sleep.

But Amy didn't sleep. Couldn't sleep.

She shouldn't be so torn about her decision. Dan

didn't give her any help, though, any clue that he might be willing to wait for her.

And was that even fair? To expect him to approve of her breezing in and out of his life as she chased her dream? Going from one assignment to the next as the opportunity presented itself?

A clean break would be best. To stay the course they'd both originally agreed on.

She'd have to deal with the attorney business when the assignment was over in two months, or have Dan get the ball rolling himself.

But how was she going to leave this child she'd come to love?

The man she'd come to love?

These people whose lives and well-being had come to mean so much to her?

Why had God handed her her heart's desire, only to dangle another in front of her, to make her choose?

Chapter Fourteen

For the first time in years, they changed the traditions for Easter Sunday in Shotgun Ridge, a direct result of Amy's innovative ideas and Emily Bodine's advertising enthusiasm.

Sunrise service on the knoll of the original Shotgun Ridge had been a sight to behold. As the sun rose over the horizon in the east, Dan had indeed preached to the masses in his signature style, with plenty of laughter and creative license with the parables he told.

Now, as they prepared for the second service of the morning, this time in the church, Amy stood by his side, holding Shayna, greeting their friends and neighbors.

"My parents made it," he murmured softly.

Amy's heart lurched. The four people walking toward them were easily recognizable. She'd seen photographs, but even without them, she would have known who they were. Dan's parents, plus his oldest brother and wife.

"Where's David?" she asked.

"He stayed in Missoula. Dad and Pip were able to get a visiting pastor to stand in for them."

So, he'd known they were coming. Odd that he hadn't said anything to her.

She was about to meet her in-laws for the first time.

On the very day she'd be packing to leave.

Oh, this was so awful. The ache in her soul was tremendous. The emptiness. A scream was building inside her. She was afraid to let it out.

Joyce Lucas enveloped her son in a warm hug, then treated Amy to the same, including the baby in the circle of her arms, laughing with a joy that mimicked Dan's trademark chortle.

"You'd be Amy, then. And this precious blessing, Shayna. I'm Joyce, the grinning hyena's mother. Irreverent boy, but one just has to love him."

Yes, one did.

"May I hold my granddaughter?" she asked, wiggling her fingers at Shayna, who obviously recognized a grandmother when she saw one, because she happily kicked her legs and nearly launched herself out of Amy's arms.

"Of course." Reluctance to let go of the child was keen. She didn't have many more hours to hold that warm little body next to her heart.

"This is my dad, Phil Lucas," Dan introduced. "And my brother, Pip, and his wife, Sally."

Phillip Jr. rolled his eyes. "Those beefy muscles are showy, but I can probably still take you."

"Here, now. There'll be no brawling on the church steps. You boys behave," Joyce said with a laugh.

Amy knew who'd ruled their household. The boys dwarfed their tiny mother, but what she lacked in stature, she made up for in inner strength. It radiated from her.

Phil Lucas stepped forward, started to hold out his hand. Amy bypassed it and gave him a hug, clinging for an extra moment. Her father had saved this man's life, set in motion a life-altering course that Amy would have otherwise missed.

Perhaps it would have been better all around if she *had* missed it. Her heart was breaking.

"It's nice to meet you, at last," Phil said. "I'm sorry to hear about your father's passing. He was a great man."

"Thank you."

She studied the family as they cooed over the baby, got reacquainted. Phil and Phillip *looked* like ministers in their tailored suits, white shirts and sedate ties. Tall and slim, there was an air of quiet reverence about them.

Nothing at all like Dan's bold presence.

The family love was so evident. They took to Shayna as though she were blood.

Having been an only child, a loner, Amy envied Dan growing up in a complete family, a father who was home for dinner each night, a mother who carried a quiet strength, worked alongside her husband, probably harder than he did. Shouldering and balancing the needs of her family with the needs of the community. She envied the siblings he'd fought with, played with, shared secrets with.

Unexpected, John White Cloud's words flashed in her mind. *You are on a journey of discovery. Answers will not come in faraway places, but inside yourself.*

Inside her was love. Everlasting love.

Dan put his hand on her shoulder, squeezed, looked down at her with an expression she couldn't read. "Ready?"

The one word seemed to foretell something much greater than the beginning of a church service. He hesitated, as though he intended to say something more, then sighed, looked around at the lawn set up for the second Easter-egg hunt that would take place later in the day, as though memorizing the terrain.

Then he ushered her inside.

Joyce didn't look ready to turn loose of Shayna, so Amy let her be. She took a seat in the second row next to Ozzie Peyton, leaving the front pew on the opposite side free for Dan's family since there was more room.

Her mind was in such a dither, she barely heard the sermon Dan delivered. It was pretty much the same message he'd given at the sunrise service, but instead of his usual trademark laughter, he was more solemn.

Shayna was a perfect angel, playing quietly in Joyce's lap. The Lucases sat with pride on their faces as they listened to their son.

Amy's attention snapped back to the pulpit when Dan fell silent. Had he lost his place again? He had a tendency to do that, and she suspected it was her fault.

"You've probably noticed that my folks are here today," he said to the congregation, "and my brother Phillip and his wife."

His eyes twinkled for a moment. Amy knew it was

taking everything inside him not to call his brother "Pip."

He lost the battle.

"Pip's agreed to step in, to take over for me while I take a bit of a sabbatical."

Murmurs rose like a swarm of locusts, buzzing, curious and confused. Amy glanced at Dan's parents. They didn't appear upset, merely watched their son with that gentle pride.

Well, of course they would. Dan had told her that they never judged him, never showed disappointment. Whatever he chose to do, they were behind him one hundred percent.

Well, she wasn't going to be so easy on him. What was the matter with him anyway? Had he lost his mind? Didn't he realize he was part of this town? Needed? He couldn't walk away.

He stepped out from behind the pulpit, walked down the steps, stopped in front of her. "Can we speak in private?"

"Are you joking? What in the world is the matter with you?"

"Well, now," Ozzie murmured from beside her. "This ought to be interesting, you bet."

Amy and Dan glared at him.

His blue eyes twinkled, but he held up his hands in surrender. "Butting out."

That'll be the day. Ozzie heard the words in his head as clear as day. Vanessa. His heart melted and he answered in kind, silently. *Are you watching, love?*

Turning back to Amy, Dan said, "Let's go somewhere and talk."

"Absolutely not. You gave up your right to privacy when you made that very public announcement. There's a room full of confused people in here. You can't just announce that you're not going to be their preacher anymore and ride off into the sunset—or whatever it is you think you're doing—"

"Damn it, Amy. I want this to be a real marriage. Forever."

She was so astonished that he'd cursed in church, she shut her mouth. Then she looked at his mother.

The woman was chuckling.

Had the whole world gone mad?

"Dan—"

"No, listen. You had your chance to speak in private. You ought to know by now that I'm at my best when there's an audience. And right now, it's vital that I be at my best."

Her heart clicked and softened at his earnest voice.

"I'm listening."

"Pip's here because I asked him to come. There's a missionary position open in Africa and I can fill in there for as long or short of a time as I want. We can go there, as a family. The three of us. Shayna and I will come with you. Follow you wherever your next assignment takes you. You can take your pictures, have your dream, but I want to be your true dream man. Your forever husband."

"Dan—"

"I'm not through. You wanted a man who would travel with you. Instead, the man you'd pinned your hopes on let you down. Your grandfather let you down with his disappointment. I want to change all that.''

He'd left out one person, she realized suddenly. Her father had let her down, too. It hit her like a bolt out of the blue.

She was pursuing her goals for the wrong reasons, chasing the wrong dream.

Being part of the upper-crust crowd back home, Amy had chafed against it, become somewhat of a rebel—just like her father.

She'd thought she was paying tribute to her dad by choosing his career and flaunting convention by working in a gentleman's club. Unconsciously, she'd been trying to gain her absent father's approval, make him *notice* her…wherever he was. Even after death.

But she realized that what she'd *really* been doing was trying to get away from judgmental people.

In the beginning when this crazy will had turned her world upside down, she'd worried that being a preacher's wife would thrust her right back into a life of more judgmental nonsense, having to keep up appearances, be someone she wasn't.

That wasn't the case at all. Mainly because Dan was so *normal*. He didn't fit any of her preconceived notions of what a minister should be like.

And these people of Shotgun Ridge accepted her unconditionally. Oh, they discussed everybody else's business, but it was more like family staying in touch with what their loved ones were going through.

Family was what she'd been searching for.

She realized that she'd spent a good part of her childhood at her grandparents' house, because the stability had made her feel safe. Gramps had always been there for her. Unlike Dad, who had let his family down.

The realization had her sucking in her breath. Oh, my gosh, why hadn't she seen this before?

Because she'd been too stubborn to look past a daughter's defense of her father, too busy defending him to the town's whispered censure—and to Gramps himself.

Yet Gramps had known all along what she needed. Family and love. He'd taken a highly unorthodox way of pushing her, a great risk, but it had worked, better than she ever imagined.

And now here was Dan.

This wonderful man standing in front of her with his heart in his eyes, offering her the world.

She didn't want the world.

She only wanted the man.

And the baby.

The sacrifice he offered touched her deeply. She'd seen how important he was to this community.

"You're not leaving, Dan. This is where you belong."

"Amy—"

"No, you've had your say, now I'll have mine. You give so much of yourself to others, put yourself last. Who's there to console *you* when somebody dies, or a kid you've tried to help goes to jail? Who's there to celebrate or encourage *your* dreams?"

She pressed her fingers to his lips when he opened them to speak.

"You love me, don't you?"

"More than the air I breathe."

She was going to weep. She knew it. She slid her hand over the lapel of his jacket, rested it against his heart.

"I may not be the ideal of preacher's-wife material, but you'll just have to deal with it. Because just as this is where you belong, it's where I belong, too. By your side."

"You *are* the ideal. Mine."

Happy tears spilled over her cheeks. Here, standing in front of her, was her true dream. No photograph or award could compete or compare.

There was a room full of strong women in this town—both wives and career women. Not one of them had given up a part of themselves for love, or sacrificed who they needed to be—who they were best at being.

Love made a woman complete.

"What about your photography?" he asked.

Answers will not come in faraway places, but inside yourself. "Oh, you'll still have to put up with a camera decorating me like a three-pound necklace. I've an idea for a book, and I've got plenty of fabulous subjects right here. The best subject of all is you, though. I love you, Dan Lucas."

He cupped her face in his hands, kissed her in front of God and the whole church.

Laughter, tears and applause roared through the church, but neither Amy or Dan paid it any mind. They had eyes only for each other.

"Well, now," Ozzie said, passing an extra handkerchief to Lloyd Brewer, who sat beside him.

"Guess old Ben Marshall knew what he was about after all, you bet." He raised his eyes heavenward, figuring he ought to give a little credit to the Man upstairs as well.

You done a good job once again. You bet. Course, it never hurts to have a willing committee down here on the ground to lend a hand in the matchmaking. You bet.

And as the preacher's wife continued to kiss her husband, well beyond what was acceptable in polite company, not a person thought to object, and there wasn't a dry eye in the bunch, either.

Epilogue

April—one year later

It was nearly one o'clock in the afternoon, mountain time. The tiny newsroom in Shotgun Ridge was packed to the rafters.

At three o'clock, eastern time, the Pulitzer board would gather to make their announcement from Columbia University's World Room.

Amy rested her hand on her pregnant stomach, noted that Dan was watching her like a hawk—or rather a nervous expectant father. She was a week past her due date. Kelly Hammond said that was normal for first babies.

Amy believed that the tiny boy in her womb knew exactly what he was waiting for—what his mother, as well as the whole town, was waiting for.

Shayna, at seventeen months, was walking now—streaking, actually. The child was happy, full of sass and vinegar, and moved faster than a six-legged jackrabbit.

"Sit down," Dan said, his tone worried. He started

to go after Shayna, but Mildred Bagley snagged the little girl.

"I can't sit. I'm as nervous as a pig in a packing house." She rubbed her extended stomach. "Probably look like one, too."

"You're beautiful," he said, putting his hand over hers, over their second child. "And you're perfect. No matter what happens today."

She smiled at him. "I know. I have everything I could ever want."

With Joe Little Coyote's permission, she'd written a feature article on him, about a medicine man who'd lost his will to live and found it again, not in healing, but in rescuing a child from a burning home. She'd portrayed the community spirit of this small town as they'd pulled together to help out families in need.

The article had run in the *Shotgun Ridge Gazette,* along with two photographs, the first one she'd taken as he sat alone on the porch, staring out of empty eyes that had given up on life, and the other of him kneeling in the rubble of ashes, hands bandaged, the nearly intact stuffed animal lying among the blackened ruins.

The instant she'd developed the photos, she'd known they were special, powerful, told a story all their own.

She could have submitted the piece to a larger, syndicated paper with a much wider audience, but she'd decided that if by some chance her work could compete with the thousands of others who would no doubt enter, she wanted her town and these people recognized as well.

This was her home.

Her true dream.

Mort Haines, the editor of the small-town paper, had been touched, and eager to accept Amy and all of Amy's work.

"Here we go," Mort said, huddled around the ticker, and Amy felt a wave of nausea swamp her. Perspiration dampened her palms, trickled between her breasts. Her internal thermostat was off since the pregnancy, and nerves made it go totally haywire. She'd been battling this ever since they'd found out she was a finalist.

"Amy, get over here," Ozzie Peyton shouted.

She shook her head wildly, pulled back when Dan started to herd her through the crowd. "I can't watch."

As the wire service sheet rolled out, Mort began reading off the Pulitzer Prize categories, the names of the winners and two finalists.

A finalist would be good, she told herself. It was recognition.

She squeezed Dan's hand so hard her knuckles ached. There were twenty-one awards out of well over two thousand entries.

The wait was agonizing.

"For a distinguished example of feature photography in black-and-white, or color…Amy Lucas!" Mort shouted.

Amy's heart leaped right into her mouth. Dan picked her up, huge belly and all, and swung her around as a roaring cheer resounded in the tiny newsroom. Opal Bagley, normally the reserved one of the sisters, kissed Henry Jenkins full on the lips.

"Congratulations, sweetheart. You did it."

Her eyes widened, the prize forgotten as warmth trickled down her legs.

"Um, Dan?"

"Yes, sweetheart?"

"Is there a doctor in the house?"

"Sure, Chance and Kelly are…" His words trailed off, his Adam's apple bobbing. "The baby?"

"I hope so. If not, I've wet my pants in all the excitement."

Her feet had hardly touched the ground before he scooped her up in his arms again, this time cradling her like a fragile piece of china about to shatter.

"Clear the way, everybody. Chance, get over here. You, too, Kelly. We're having a baby."

You'd think nobody else in the room had ever experienced such a joy. He was a nervous wreck. She had to smile.

"Dan?"

"What?"

"I can walk."

He seemed to realize he was overreacting a bit. He laughed. "Yeah, but you know how I like to show off my manly muscles."

She raised a brow. "Those manly muscles are partly responsible for me being in this condition. You were just too hard to resist."

He laughed. "Have a care for telling our personal business in a room full of big ears. You're the preacher's wife."

"That I am. And proud of it."

He gazed down at her. "And I'm proud of you. Congratulations, sweetheart. I wanted to be the man standing by your side when you won this award. I got my wish."

"And I got mine. And the man."

* * * * *

*We hope you've enjoyed your
stay in Shotgun Ridge!
Don't miss Mindy Neff's next story,*

DELIVERED WITH A KISS,

in Harlequin American Romance's
MAITLAND MATERNITY
collection entitled

THE McCALLUM QUINTUPLETS.

*Available February 2002
at a store near you.*

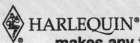

Coming in December from

HARLEQUIN®

AMERICAN *Romance*®

MAITLAND MATERNITY

Triplets, Quads & Quints:
Multiple births lead to
remarkable love stories.

When Maitland Maternity Hospital opens a new
multiple-birth wing donated by the McCallum family,
unforgettable surprises are sure to follow. Don't miss the
fun, the romance, the joy…as the McCallum triplets find
love just outside the delivery-room door.

Watch for:

TRIPLET SECRET BABIES
by Judy Christenberry
December 2001

QUADRUPLETS ON THE DOORSTEP
by Tina Leonard
January 2002

THE McCALLUM QUINTUPLETS
(3 stories in 1 volume)
featuring *New York Times* bestselling author Kasey Michaels,
Mindy Neff and Mary Anne Wilson
February 2002

Available at your favorite retail outlet.

HARLEQUIN®
Makes any time special®

Visit us at www.eHarlequin.com

HARMAIT